Also by Michael K. Hill

Anansi and Beyond:

Short Stories, Magic, & Nightmares

A DIFFERENT TIME

Michael K. Hill

TANGENT PRESS EAST

Published by
Tangent Press East
Tangent Entertainment, LLC
14 Ciccio Court
Plainville, CT 06062

This novel is a work of fiction. Names, characters, places, and incidents are the product of the author's imagination or are used fictionally. Any resemblance to actual persons, living or dead, events or locales is entirely coincidental.

ISBN: 9781099118531

Book design by Nick Salvo

Author photo by Rachelle Cardone-Hill

Cover design by Ana Voicu

First Edition

July 2019

For Beth,

my soulmate.

Prologue

New York, New York
March 3, 2007, 11:09 AM

A fine dusting of light snow floated onto West 40th Street and Broadway, coating parked cars like powdered sugar, while tendrils of steam escaped from storm drains, then vanished in the chilly air. For a 10-year-old Keith Nolan, it was his first visit to Manhattan, and it felt he'd been waiting for it his whole life.

Before this trip, his only experiences with The Big Apple occurred in the primary colors of comic book pages. But seeing it in person, the city was wondrous. Every street held mysteries, each building buzzed with life. Keith decided at that moment he wanted to live in New York when he grew up.

He knew it was silly and understood the stuff in his comics wasn't real, but it didn't change the fact he wanted to see a superhero in person. Keith craned his neck back and scanned the skyscrapers, in awe of the towering steel and glass monsters, stretching to infinity.

"They're tall, huh?" his father asked.

Keith's parents walked a few steps behind him, hand in hand, bundled up against the chilly weather. His mom wore a long red overcoat with black mittens, cap, and a scarf wrapped twice around her neck, hiding half her face. His father had a dark gray, heavy wool pea coat and a well-worn Yankees cap.

"Are we getting close?" Keith shouted over his shoulder.

"We're getting close," his father said.

Keith's eyes widened and a happy grin spread across his face. He picked up his pace as they weaved through the crowded sidewalk. He'd anticipated this trip for months and counted down each day on his Marvel Comics wall calendar. The month of March featured Spider-man swinging high above Times Square, which seemed perfect.

"And I can get anything I want?" Keith called back as he shuffled around a hot dog vendor's cart.

"*Anything* you want," his father said. "It's your birthday."

"*Anything* under fifty dollars," his mother mumbled through her scarf.

In the street, taxi cabs zipped in and out of traffic like giant, metal insects, communicating with angry horn blasts.

The family's destination was the largest comic book shop in the Tri-state area. Its legend made grander by his father's stories of the store's sheer size and magnificence. He'd reminisce about spending an entire day browsing through three floors of comic books, memorabilia, and magic.

Keith's legs moved faster, kicking up swirls of snow with each step.

Behind him, his mother clung to her husband's arm for warmth. She tapped him and they paused for a moment as she pointed with excitement at a store window. He pulled his wife closer and kissed the top of her capped head while they admired the display.

But Keith kept moving, now focused on the red brick building emerging through the snow, one block ahead. Even at that distance, he could already see the huge superheroes banner, hanging from the second floor windows, waving in the icy air. Excitement coursed through his veins as his mind raced with the potential treasures waiting inside. Keith charged into the intersection without slowing.

He never saw the red DONT WALK sign.

Halfway across Keith heard the horrible sound of locked brakes and screeching tires. He turned to his right and saw an enormous delivery truck sliding on the snow, straight toward him.

Frozen to the spot, Keith could only watch as the truck bore down. In that instant, he saw the horrified expression on the driver and focused instead on the oncoming stainless steel grill and how it glistened with drops of melted snow.

He tensed for the impact.

Then someone grabbed his hand and yanked him out of the street. The momentum caused him to stumble back and collapse onto the sidewalk, just as the truck skidded to a stop— six feet passed where he had stood.

Keith's breath came in rapid, short bursts as his heart hammered in his chest. Blinking, he sensed a presence behind him to the left. He spun in that direction and saw the person who plucked him out of the intersection.

Dressed in a bright yellow rain slicker with the hood pulled up, a pale and gaunt woman in her mid-thirties stared at him. One hand covered her mouth, while the other extended to Keith, fingers splayed.

He looked up at her, dumbfounded.

In that instant he felt recognition. He knew her face.

"Are you okay?" she quivered, as tears welled in her eyes. "Did I hurt you?"

Keith shook his head. "No, you saved me."

A nervous laugh escaped her as a single tear slipped down her cheek. "I feared I wouldn't reach you in time."

The truck driver cranked down his window and shouted down to them. "Jesus Christ, kid, watch where you're going! You're lucky she saw you, or you would have been road pizza." He scowled, shifted the truck into gear, and drove off.

A crowd gathered around Keith, as his parents, wild with fear, pushed through the gathering and rushed to their son. His mom knelt beside him and clutched his coat. *"Never do that again, Keith,"* she said, in a harsh whisper.

"Thank God you're okay," his father said.

"You should thank her," Keith said and pointed at the woman in the raincoat.

Keith's mom turned toward her. "Did you pull him out of the way?"

The woman smiled. "I'm happy I saw him in time."

His mother's expression shifted from appreciation to astonishment, as recognition dawned. "Wait, wait. I *know* you," she gasped. "You're Edith Kinsley."

The woman smiled and nodded.

Keith's mom stood and stepped toward her, opening her arms. Edith accepted the gesture and hugged her back. After a moment they released. Keith's mom turned to her son and husband, her cheeks streaked with tears. She pointed at the woman in the raincoat and said, "Can you believe it?"

Keith's father looked puzzled.

"This is Edith Kinsley. She's the author of *The Adventures of Oba and Nim.*"

His confusion continued.

Keith's mother narrowed her eyes and crossed her arms. "It was your son's favorite book when he was little. I read it to him all the time."

"Oh," he said, nodding.

Keith stood up and brushed off the snow. "I knew I recognized you," he said to Edith. "You're the lady on the back of the book."

His mother turned to Edith. "How can we ever thank you?"

Edith smiled. "You've shared my book with your child. That's all the thanks I need." She bent down to Keith and tousled his hair. "Were you running to the comic book store?"

"How did you know?"

"Lucky guess."

Keith burst into a grin. "Today is my birthday."

"It is?" Edith opened her purse and took out a ten-dollar bill.

Keith's parents both protested.

"Nonsense," Edith said. She handed the bill to Keith. "Happy birthday, young man. Use that to buy a few comics. Who knows, maybe someday you'll be a writer, and people will buy *your* books." Then she stood up and snapped closed her purse. "Very nice to meet you all."

"Thank you, again," his mother said.

Edith nodded, turned and walked away, disappearing into the falling snow.

Chapter 1

On a bright October morning, Keith Nolan entered a flea market in Hoboken, New Jersey. He hid behind a pair of brown turtle shell glasses that his mom once told him matched his coffee-colored eyes. 22-years-old, thin, with short sandy-blond hair, and pale skin from too much time spent parked in front of a computer screen, his goal that Saturday morning was to browse collectibles. Instead, his entire life was about to change.

Every Saturday morning he would ride his bike, alone, to an old, former factory just a few blocks from the banks of the Hudson River. Converted into a makeshift retail outlet, vendors from around the region displayed their wares for eager shoppers. The most common items included baseball cards, maps, porcelain figurines, vinyl albums, vintage toys, watches, books, and second-hand clothes.

He reveled roaming the market, scouring tables in search of treasures, and breathing air tinged with the aroma of time. Keith was a massive anime fan with a penchant for classic video games, but his highest ambition was completing a personal collection of comic books from the 1970s and 80s. To flip through stacks of comics in long, immaculate white storage boxes, hoping to find an issue he needed, made Keith swoon. It was his true love.

As he strolled through the market, he glanced up seeing the morning sunlight glinting through the cracked window panes lining the upper perimeter of the old factory. He was gazing at those windows when he walked right into someone. Startled, Keith apologized before recognizing who he hit.

"Keith Nolan?" the young man said. "Holy shit, dude, I haven't seen you since high school. It's Todd Schafer, remember?" Then, without warning, he punched Keith in the gut. It wasn't full force, but enough to double him over. Todd laughed. "Your reflexes *still* suck, man!"

Keith stood back up and grimaced. "Hi, Todd."

Todd was tall, with an artificial tan, and slicked hair pulled into a man bun like a pseudo-samurai.

"I didn't hurt you, did I?" Todd said, and then patted Keith on the head. "So what's up? What are you doing in Jersey?"

"I live here," Keith said.

"Terrific," Todd said with no sincerity. "I'm just slumming for the weekend. I work in Manhattan. It's pretty sweet. Hey, are you and Skyler still together?"

Keith broke eye contact and looked at his shoes.

"No," he said after a moment.

"Bummer, man. She was fucking hot! Do you have her number?" he cackled, before glancing at his watch. "Hey, we should totally get together some time, catch up over a few beers. I could show you all the cool shit I'm doing." He reached into his jacket, pulled out a glossy business card and handed it to Keith. "Call me. It'll be fun!"

Keith attempted a smile and nodded.

Todd walked away, and as he disappeared from view, Keith dropped the card in the trash and resumed his journey through the market.

The encounter with Todd had dampened Keith's mood. He hadn't thought of people from high school for over a year– Skyler in particular. But being reminded of her left him nauseous. He'd been sure he'd stashed those feelings in the deepest recesses of his mind.

From off to his right, someone called his name.

"Happy Saturday, Keith," said one vendor, a grizzled old man with thinning white hair and a crooked smile. He wore a faded New Jersey Devils sweatshirt and jeans wearing thin at the knees.

"Hey, Stu," Keith said.

"You look like you ate bad sushi," said Stu. "You all right?"

Keith waved a hand, dismissing the notion. "I'm fine."

Stu's tables specialized in home video, selling laserdiscs, VHS videotapes, DVDs, and even Blu-rays, but he also offered novels, magazines, and occasionally comic books.

"Anything new this week?" Keith asked, looking over the items displayed on the tables.

"No new comics, I'm sorry to say. But I got a fresh box of vintage VHS tapes. Could be a surprise lurking in there for you. Maybe some of that Japanese crap you're so fond of."

Stu hunted through the stacks of bins and boxes piled high behind the table.

"Did you ever finish writing that superhero story you told me about?" Stu glanced at Keith over his shoulder as he shuffled cartons.

"Nah," said Keith. "It wasn't very good."

"You should keep at it. I bet you'd be great." Stu located the crate he wanted, an over-sized box on the floor, and bent to pick it up. As he hoisted it, he groaned and almost toppled over backward. Keith grabbed Stu's shoulders to steady him.

"Let me help you with that," Keith said, picking up the crate.

A flush spread across Stu's cheeks. "Maybe it's time I use smaller boxes. Thanks, kiddo. You may have saved me a busted hip."

Keith smiled. "No problem."

He placed the container on top of the last table and sorted through the contents. Most included a protective sleeve, providing the name of the movie and its stars, but a few were bare, with only a label to identify them. Nothing caught his eye. Most were cheesy action movies from the 80s or episodes of *Blue's Clues*. He was preparing to abandon the search when he spotted something odd at the bottom of the box.

It was half the size of the regular tapes, a format known as VHS-C used in camcorders, not commercial movies. Around the perimeter of the label was an ornate, intricate, hand-drawn lattice. In the middle, written with a delicate, feminine style, it read: *Tape #3.*

Keith pulled the tape out of the box and held it for a moment, feeling an almost imperceptible vibration radiating from it. He held the tape up to show Stu.

"What about this one?" Keith asked.

"I don't even know what that is," Stu said. "It's probably a video of a kid's birthday party or something."

"How much do you want for it?"

Stu smiled his crooked grin again. "From you? Take it! It's the least I can do for stopping me from falling on my ass."

Keith stood and tucked the small tape into his coat pocket, then pushed the heavy box below the table. "Thanks, Stu," he said. "See you next week."

As he worked his way around the rest of the market, it annoyed Keith to find his mind returning to Todd. *I should have thrown that card in his face and told him to piss off,* Keith thought.

He pushed his hands into his pockets and felt the tape he'd received from Stu. The contact produced a tingling sensation in his fingertips that relaxed him.

Screw it. Why waste time on the past?

He was pondering the videotape's origin when he spotted an unfamiliar comic book vendor with an extensive display spanning multiple tables. Keith's heart rate elevated as his hands slipped out of his pockets and explored the first row in a series of long boxes filled with vintage books.

Keith flipped through the stacks and made small talk with the seller, a wiry, dark-haired guy with a goatee and blue-tinted glasses.

"New here?" Keith asked.

"Yeah, my first week. Most of the time I'm in Newark, but I decided to try this place. You come here often?"

But Keith ignored him. His entire attention focused on what he held in his hands. For Keith, it was the Holy Grail, a comic book he'd been searching for his whole life.

His passion for comic books began on his tenth birthday, a few years before his parents died. That year his dad presented him with a massive stack of *Uncanny X-Men*, a collection his father had been building since the 70's.

There were several gaps, missing books that prevented it from being a *complete* collection, but over the years, Keith had acquired each one and added them to the group. But, one book remained elusive - a rare issue from 1979, #117 - and with a stunned expression frozen on his face, he stared in disbelief as he held it in his hands. The copy was pristine, and the bright, vibrant colors of the cover were mesmerizing. His heart raced, and his mouth hung open.

The vendor noticed Keith's reaction, stepped closer, and allowed himself a wry smile. "Find something?"

"What's the price of this issue?" Keith asked just above a whisper.

"That's a valuable book, son."

"How much?"

"In that condition, I'd want $210."

"Do you take credit cards?"

●

Keith peddled through the bustling streets of his neighborhood, with the crisp autumn air chilling his skin as his mind raced. Everything blurred passed him—the people bundled in sweaters and hats, navigating taxis swerving to avoid him, and the trees lining the sidewalk, bursting with Fall colors of red and gold. His thoughts fixated only on the prize now stashed in his backpack.

When he arrived at his apartment, he locked his bike on the rack and sprinted up the cement steps into the lobby. Too impatient to wait for the elevator, he dashed up the stairwell to the second floor and down the hallway to his door.

His fingers numb from gripping the handlebars, he fumbled with the keys. When the lock opened, he stepped into the darkened apartment, pulled off the backpack, leaning it against his legs, and removed his jacket, tossing it onto the cluttered couch.

With the backpack, Keith rushed into his bedroom, past his unmade bed, and knelt beside the stacks of long boxes kept next to the wall which held his comic collection. He shifted them around, searching for a specific box. When he found it, he removed the lid with reverence. Inside were the oldest books, the ones from his father. He gently flipped through the titles.

He stopped for a moment on issue #101. As he touched the cover, he remembered his father imparting the details of how he bought it at the town drugstore, against the protestations of the elderly woman behind the counter who thought he shouldn't be wasting time on rubbish. His dad had responded by telling her he'd buy whatever he wanted and then paid the cover price of thirty-cents with money earned from his paper route. Next, Keith stopped at issue #113, a gift from his parents on his fourteenth birthday, the last time they were together. He fought back the tears and kept moving through the pile until he found the section he was looking for, between issues #116 and #118.

He unzipped the backpack and—with meticulous care—extracted the book from the plain brown bag, gazing on it in wonder, before easing it into its new home.

"I've got them all now, Dad," he whispered.

He wiped at his eyes with his sleeve and replaced the cover. On the floor, with his hands resting on the boxes, Keith allowed the memories to wash over him.

After several minutes, he stood, regained his composure, and removed the cell phone from his back pocket. He pressed the contacts button, and a brief list of numbers appeared — his job, Pizza delivery, Chinese food, Mexican food, and at the top of the list, his buddy, Aric. He pressed that link.

The call answered on the second ring.

"Hey, man," said Aric. "What's up?"

"Are you doing anything?" Keith asked.

"Trolling on Reddit," he said. "Can you believe some assholes don't consider *Die Hard* a Christmas movie?"

"Come over. I have something to show you."

"See ya in ten."

Keith carried the long boxes into the living room, setting them side by side on the floor in front of the couch and removing the covers. He picked up the empty pizza boxes and threw them in the trash. Then bundled the dirty clothes into a ball and tossed them in the bedroom, closing the door. Keith returned to the living room, sat on the rocker-recliner, turned on the TV and Xbox and resumed playing *Cuphead* while he waited for his friend.

He'd met Aric a year earlier when he first moved to Hoboken. He'd been exploring the local comic shop when a pudgy Viking, heavy-set, with a full beard, and longish hair, bumped into him by accident, spilling the pile of books Keith was holding. Instead of being a dick, Aric got on his knees and helped gather the scattered comics. He spotted issue #147 of *Uncanny X-Men*, held it up to Keith, and said, "Such a great book." Then he dropped his voice to a conspiratorial level and whispered, "I have an extra copy of this one. It's mint. I'll sell it to you for half of that," he said, pointing to the price.

A smile spread across Keith's face. He had been living in Hoboken for six months and was starting to think he was the only guy in town who even knew what a comic book was.

They exchanged contact information and from that day had been friends.

●

Ten minutes later there was a knock on the door.

"It's open," Keith called from his chair.

Aric entered, wearing an olive green army jacket and a wool hat. As he stepped into the apartment, he spotted the open comic boxes, and Keith seated beside them, beaming.

"What is this?" he asked, pulling off his hat and coat.

"Check it out," Keith said, gesturing to the boxes.

Aric's brow furrowed and a look of disbelief spread across his face. "Did you do it? Did you finally do it?"

Keith only smiled.

Aric rushed over to the first box, kneeling in front of it, he flipped through the stack with purpose. When he found what he was searching for, he removed it and held it up in front of him like Indiana Jones gazing at the Golden Idol.

"Holy shit, dude. You did it? You completed the collection?"

Keith nodded, still grinning.

"That's so awesome, man. Congrats!" Aric stood and bear-hugged Keith. "Where did you find it?"

"The flea market," Keith said.

Aric handed him the book with great care.

"How much?"

"Don't ask," Keith said with a chuckle. "More than I wanted to pay, but I couldn't pass it up."

"Ever heard of negotiating?" Aric asked.

"It was too late. The guy knew by my reaction I wanted it."

"Dude, how many times have I told you to work on your poker face? One look at you and the entire world knows what you're thinking."

"It doesn't matter. I got it, and the collection is complete."

"I'm happy for you, man," Aric said. "We should celebrate. Chinese food?"

They enjoyed a meal at Mr. Foo's, an Asian restaurant around the corner from the apartment. Keith ordered beef and broccoli. Aric got General Tso's chicken and a pupu plater for himself. The place was empty except for them. The only sounds were soft, bubbling water coming from the artificial fish pond and mini waterfall near the register.

Aric wiped his face with a napkin, but parts of his beard were still slick with sauce. "Since you've completed your collection, I expect a significant amount of mad money will now be available to you. Is a girlfriend next? Because I know how that works, kemosabe. I become the third wheel, feeling awkward, sitting on the couch while you two suck face. That type of thing can be very distracting, especially if I'm in the middle of beating Forest Fortress on *Mario World*." He took a sip of his beer. "So you aren't planning to date are you?"

"No," Keith said. "Look around us. Do you see any women interested in me?"

"Dude, if you applied yourself, you could *most definitely* find a girl. I'm asking you *not* to."

"What do you mean, 'applied' myself?" Keith asked.

"For example, not hanging around with me."

"That's crazy," Keith said, and then noticed bits of a fortune cookie collected on Aric's chest.

"Nah, it's cool," Aric said. "It's true. I'm a chick repellent. But I enjoy hanging with you, and I'd hate to lose that."

"Well, shut up, because it's not happening."

Aric's face broke into a broad smile, and he hoisted up his can of beer. "Awesome!"

Basking in the day's excitement and content after a meal shared with his friend, Keith had forgotten about the unique videotape still sitting in his pocket.

Chapter 2

In the spring of 1989, Lindsey Hale was 19 years old and sure of only one thing—how happy she was high school had finished. Since graduating the previous June, she'd existed in a fog, indecisive about her future. She wanted only to find her way without interference from others. Lindsey was 16 when her parents divorced, and her mother yanked her from the Elysium of Oahu, Hawaii to move 2500 miles away to Visalia, California. Her father remained behind in paradise, while her mom dragged her to a new state, a new school, and a whole new life.

The results were not surprising. Lindsey found fitting in with a group of kids who had known each other since elementary school difficult. She arrived as an outsider and stayed one. She coped with the loneliness by immersing herself in her art—sketching, painting, and writing stories in most of her free time. Whatever time remained she spent curled up on the couch, buried in a book.

Lindsey stepped out of the shower as heavy steam filled the bathroom and covered the mirror with condensation. With a towel, she dried her long dark hair before pulling it back into a ponytail and securing it with a black hair tie. She wasn't a fan of mousse, gel, hairspray, or the rest, preferring a more simplistic, natural look.

She pulled on her bathrobe and exited with a warm trail of vapor lingering behind her as she walked down the canary yellow hallway to her bedroom. Everything in her mother's house was a variation of yellow.

From the kitchen, her mother called out to her.

"Lindsey, we're having breakfast. Want to join us?"

"No, thanks, mom," she said before closing her door.

Lindsey's cramped room had a twin bed positioned in the corner, under the window, looking out at the street. On the opposite wall sat a matching dresser, with a cassette tape deck and record player resting on top of it. The walls featured framed displays of her artistic endeavors, realistic sketches of enormous trees extending into infinity.

She pulled a paisley sundress with thin shoulder straps over her slim frame and stepped into an old pair of flip-flops. From her nightstand, she picked up a sketching pad, several pencils, her Walkman with orange foam headphones, and a cassette tape decorated with ornate, hand-drawn lattice around the edge. Its label read: MY MIX #6, in a delicate, feminine style.

In the hallway, she stopped at the closet and removed a light jacket from the rack. She hoped she could pass through the kitchen without having to engage in the routine morning bicker with her mom, but knew it was a pipe dream.

"Where are you off to, so early?" her mother asked as Lindsey entered the kitchen, making a beeline for the back door.

Phyllis Udell-Herring, her maiden name now hyphenated with her second husband's surname, stood at the kitchen sink washing dishes. She was an alluring woman in her late 40's, with blond hair styled short and spiked on the top. Despite a somewhat liberal application of foundation and concealer, the morning sunlight revealed a series of wrinkles creeping into the corners of her eyes and mouth.

Lindsey's step-father, Wit, sat at the kitchen table, scanning the newspaper. A skinny man with a gaunt face and recessed eyes, he had thinning hair, cut in a military buzz. Faded tattoos covered his bony arms.

Both looked at Lindsey as if she were a specimen on display in a laboratory.

"You're not going to work dressed like that are you? I thought we agreed you would wear that Evan Picone dress I got you at Fashion Bug? Didn't she look lovely in that, Wit?"

He shrugged without looking up from the paper.

"They cut my hours," Lindsey said. "I guess they're overstaffed right now."

"When do you work again?" Phyllis asked.

"I don't know. I'll get a call when I'm needed."

"So we're back to Wit and I being the only people earning a paycheck in this house? What do you plan to do for money?"

"I have a little bit saved up," Lindsey said.

"If you don't have work, where are you going? Dressed that way, I'll assume it's not a job interview."

"I'm going to the park to sketch."

Her mother shook her head and sighed. "Oh, Lindsey. What is the point of that nonsense?" She crossed from the sink to the kitchen table, placing a hand on Wit's shoulder. "They call them *starving artists* for a reason. Isn't that so, Wit?"

"What is the point?" Wit parroted, through a mouthful of toast.

Lindsey took a moment to gain her composure. If she showed her anger, it guaranteed a fight.

"I find it calming and relaxing there," she said in a neutral tone.

"Is living rent-free and jobless so stressful?" her mother asked.

Lindsey smiled. "Bye, mom," she said and opened the kitchen door.

"Say goodbye to your step-father."

"Goodbye, *Wit,*" she said.

"Will you be home for supper?" her mother called after her, but Lindsey had closed the door.

She seethed with anger as she walked to her car. In the driver's seat of the lemon yellow, 4-door Nissan Maxima, she paused a moment and resisted the urge to pound the steering wheel. After several deep breaths, she started the engine and headed west toward Highway 198.

●

Visalia was a picturesque city, but for Lindsey, it always paled compared to Hawaii. The one saving grace was its proximity to Sequoia National Park. Situated among the Sierra Nevada Mountains, and only a fifty-minute drive from her home, the park was the protected home to the giant sequoia trees growing in the shadow of Mount Whitney.

Lindsey cranked open the window, popped the cassette tape into the stereo and cranked up the volume. Warm air and the sound of Belouis Some's "Imagination" washed over her. She relaxed.

At the park entrance, she maneuvered the car into a shaded spot and killed the engine. She picked up her sketch pad and pencils, exited the vehicle and headed out to walk among the giants.

The park was her refuge, her escape from the tension and pressure imposed by her mother and the uncertainty of her future. When she sat at the base of the mammoth trees, sketching their grandeur and communing with nature, she found peace and tranquility.

She sat in the warm dirt, looking up in amazement as the trees stretched into the heavens. Some of the Sequoias reached heights over two hundred feet with a girth of twenty feet in diameter. Seated at their base, Lindsey felt dwarfed and insignificant. She approached one of them and placed her hands on the massive tree, feeling the soft, dense, bark against her skin. She closed her eyes and imagined the passing centuries since the tree's birth.

With her sketchbook open, she drew an approximation of her view, before stopping, hanging her head and clutching her arms.

She knew she faced choices concerning her future, and she dreaded them. Her mother wanted her to either find a job or a husband. Prospects for the former were limited, and the latter, non-existent. She had caught the eye of several young men and even accepted a few dinner dates. But with each encounter, the incompatibility became obvious.

One was a boy from school named Billy, who played on the football team and the wrestling squad. When she asked him what he liked to read, he responded, "Reading is stupid."

Next was Blayze, a golden-god surfer from Santa Monica, who told her he was looking for a girl who could sew because most of his shirts ripped under the arms because of his, "massive biceps." When Lindsey pointed out he could sew his clothes, he laughed at her. "I'm not a fag," he said.

But the worst was a date with a college guy last fall. They had met at an INXS concert in Bakersfield. He seemed like a nice guy, smart, polite, and good-looking. Their dinner was going well, and both commented on it. He asked if she was going to college, and she shrugged.

"Good," he said. "I'm not looking for a woman with career plans." The statement stunned her. The truth was she didn't have a clue *what* she wanted to do, but the notion he opposed it, infuriated her. Without another word she stood and walked to their waiter, handing him money for her meal and then left the restaurant.

She hadn't dated since.

The more she considered it, the less interested in the prospect she became. Life had provided her with a front-row seat to the destructive nature of marriage. Her parents had fought incessantly. The endless barrage of nagging and belittling comments from her mother drove a giant wedge between them until her father finally stopped speaking to Phyllis. The divorce soon followed.

Now her mother was with husband number two, a man devoid of personality and charisma, present in her mother's life for the simple reason he represented a steady paycheck. Lindsey knew her mother didn't love him, but she'd forgo such foolishness for comfort and stability.

Lindsey had no interest in that.

If she had a soulmate, she knew the attraction would be undeniable, and he'd never feel threatened by her voicing an opinion. But if such a person didn't exist, she decided she was okay with that too.

She closed her eyes and recited a mantra, "*Sail to serenity. Sail to serenity.*" As she repeated the words, the pressures of the world faded, and she imagined an older version of herself with streaks of gray working back from her temples, in stark contrast to the rest of her dark hair. She saw a sparkle in her eyes, radiating the contentment in her heart. She pictured this in her mind.

The dream of returning to Hawaii never left her. But her father sold their old house as part of the divorce settlement and moved in with his girlfriend, Gwen. Lindsey asked to visit her father as a graduation present, but Gwen rejected the plan, having Lindsey's dad explain the apartment was too small for three adults, even for just a week. He apologized and promised to have her visit once he had his place.

So instead of a trip back to Hawaii as her graduation gift, she got her mother's old car, a ten-year-old, leaky clunker she was forced to park on the street because the puddles it left were ruining the driveway.

"It will be okay," she whispered to herself. "Even if I'm alone, I can still be happy. I only wish I had someone to talk to."

She considered solutions to that problem and decided a journal could get her focused on her choices for the future. She knew talking was easier than writing, but with no one to listen to her ramblings, she determined a diary was the best answer and committed to begin one that night.

●

By the time Lindsey returned home, the setting sun had chased pink and yellow streaks of light into the sky over the roof of her mother's house. She had a tightening pressure in her chest as she parked in front of the house. She noticed with a sense of relief that Wit's car was missing, but her mother's new Buick Century was in the garage.

As she unlocked the front door and stepped into the living room, she prepared for the next verbal assault from her mother, but to her surprise, the house was quiet and empty. A note sat on the kitchen table, explaining that Phyllis and Wit had gone out to eat. It said they had waited for Lindsey so she could join them but decided at 6:30 to let her fend for herself. "Leftovers are in the fridge," it concluded.

She crumpled the note and tossed it in the trash, then headed to the hallway closet to hang up her jacket. As she did, she spotted a small canvas bag pushed into the back corner of the closet, covered with a fine layer of dust. She removed it and set it on the hallway floor, unzipping it. Inside she found the video camera her dad had purchased back in Hawaii to record their home movies. Though it'd been just a few years, it felt like a lifetime ago.

An idea struck her. Instead of maintaining a handwritten journal, she could record a video diary. She needed to talk, and the camera could listen. It was the perfect solution.

She grabbed the bag and hurried to her room.

With the door closed, she emptied the contents onto her bed. It included the camera, a small VHS-C camcorder, the power supply/charger, two battery packs, a small tripod, and several blank tapes.

She grabbed the tripod first, extending the legs to full length and placing it in the corner of her room. She picked up the camera and snapped a battery into position.

The camcorder was a technological marvel, condensing a color video camera, tape recording unit, microphone, and an LCD playback screen into something that fit in her palm. With multiple switches covering the outside, it took Lindsey a few moments to find the power button. When she pressed it, nothing happened. She removed the battery, reseated it, and tried the switch again, but nothing powered up. She took that pack out and installed the other one. No luck.

"Shit," she mumbled to herself, then spotted the power supply. She plugged one end into the wall outlet and the other into the camera and saw the display illuminated, providing her a view of her bare feet and her bedroom floor. A message flashed: "NO TAPE."

Lindsey unwrapped one of the blank tapes, then hit the eject button that popped open the loading mechanism. She fumbled with the tape for a moment, trying to decide which way to insert it. Once she figured it out, she closed the loading door and heard the camera threading the tape into position. The on-screen message now read, "READY."

She mounted the camera on the tripod and used the zoom controls to give it a full view of her room. Then she pressed the record button, and the display showed a flashing red dot and "REC" in the upper right corner.

She stepped out from behind the camera, walked to her bed and sat on the mattress.

With her eyes closed, she took a deep breath and opened them again.

"My name is Lindsey," she said. "I need someone to talk to, and I've decided it should be you," she smiled, as a sense of calm washed over her.

Chapter 3

For ten years Keith's weekend routine hadn't changed. Every Saturday and Sunday morning he'd roll out of bed and embark on a journey to any yard sale, flea market, or comic shop he discovered, pursuing the superhero books to complete his collection. For his amusement, he imagined himself as a knight on a quest or a detective following clues.

Keith awoke that Sunday morning and experienced a frightening moment when for a second he imagined the events of the previous day had been nothing but a dream. But a quick glance at the stack of long boxes beside the bed, reorganized the night before, reassured him. Keith grinned before stretching long and catlike, realizing he had a free Sunday morning to do something different for a change.

After a quick shower, he dressed in a sweatshirt and jeans. He grabbed his coat from the rumpled pile where he tossed it the night before.

Outside the apartment, the street sparkled below a cloudless azure sky. Keith unlocked his bike, hopped on, and headed east down 14th street, toward the river, resisting the urge to revisit the flea market. The autumn air was crisp and invigorating, and the persistent pedaling raised his heart rate and cleared his head. Contentment permeated his consciousness. He smiled at strangers and wished them a good morning.

Near the end of 14th street, he saw the shimmering surface of the Hudson River and the magnificent Manhattan skyline beyond it, glistening in the daybreak.

On Frank Sinatra Drive, Keith rolled up beside a bench overlooking the pier and parked his bike. He walked to the edge of the water and gazed at the view. Around him he noticed several couples walking together, holding hands and his contentment slipped away.

Satisfaction had enveloped him only minutes earlier, but once the elation eased, the question dominating his thoughts became *what now?*

How would he fill the empty hours of his life?

For twelve years his singular purpose had been completing his father's comic collection. With that goal achieved what would he do next? Surrender to video games and Netflix binges?

A realization dawned on him. It was like pulling a curtain away and revealing something hidden. His focus on the comics was an act of misdirection, like a magician's illusion. The relentless quest kept him from confronting the truth about his life: he had no plan for his future.

He searched his thoughts for an answer, but it felt like stumbling through a thick mist. Nothing was clear. Everything was obscured.

He turned back to the skyscrapers of New York City and slid his hands into his coat pockets to warm them. He felt something. He removed it and realized it was the videotape from Stu. As he held it, he again sensed the strange tingling sensation in his fingers tips. Who made that intricate and detailed label? What was it doing in a box of old movies, and what could the recording be? He decided he wanted answers.

Keith pushed the tape back into his pocket, jogged to his bike and hopped on, pedaling fast back up 14th street.

At his apartment, he rushed over to the video equipment rack in the corner of the living room. He used the gear to convert anime programs on tape to digital files viewable on his computer or phone. It included an ancient Sony CRT monitor, a DVD burner, and an old Panasonic VHS deck. But the tape in his pocket was too small to play in a standard VCR and required an adapter. Keith knew he had one, but couldn't find it in the equipment rack. He spent the next twenty minutes ransacking the apartment looking for it. He checked under the furniture, on the movie shelf, in the closet, and under the bed, but kept coming up empty. The final place left to search was his desk.

He pulled open the drawer, peered inside, and spotted a pile of fading photographs of him and Skyler. On top of the stack sat a small jewelry flip box, covered in black velvet. He placed the box on the desktop, glanced back at the images, and his stomach tightened as he wondered why he hadn't thrown them away.

"What am I keeping these for?" he said out loud.

He grabbed the stack and pulled them out of the drawer. When he did, the photos slipped from his hands and cascaded to the floor, surrounding him with the memories of their time together. Snapshots of Skyler at the river in summer, the two of them floating on inner-tubes and smiling for the camera. There were pictures taken in her room, with them snuggled together, the bliss on their young, vibrant faces, full of joy, and ignorant of what the future held. As he gathered up the snapshots, he sensed a dull ache, like seared flesh whose pain lingers long after a burn.

Keith tossed the pile into the wastebasket beside the desk, and dropped into the chair, with a knot in his stomach. He glanced at the open drawer and spotted something lurking at the far back: the adapter. He snatched it and dashed back into the living room.

The adapter was identical in size to a regular VHS tape but featured a pop-up door to accept the smaller cassette. He loaded the videotape from Stu into it, and the adapter whirred as gears turned, threading the tape into position. When it finished, he slipped the adapter into the VCR, and auto-play engaged. Keith sat in front of the flickering monitor, his leg bouncing in anticipation, and waited several moments for an image to appear. He wasn't even sure why he was so nervous. He just knew he was. But the screen only displayed static. He sat back and sighed. After contemplating so many possibilities for what he'd find on the tape, he'd never once considered it might be blank. Then his machine made a clicking sound, stopped and switched into rewind mode.

Be kind, rewind, he thought and smiled. Whoever watched it last hadn't bothered.

When it finished, he pressed play again.

Static filled the screen, flashed, and Keith leaned in closer. An image appeared of a bedroom with yellow walls decorated with stunning framed sketches of giant trees. He saw a small bed with a flower-patterned bedspread alongside a nightstand with objects on it, but they were hard to identify. The picture resolution was low, typical of a half-century old video format. Then the image jumped as someone bumped the camera, and the sound of footsteps came through the speakers, as a young woman emerged with wild, flowing dark hair, dressed in a baggy INXS concert t-shirt and gray sweatpants. She wore no makeup and yet her face was radiant. She positioned herself on the edge of the bed, shrugged and smiled at the camera.

"Here we are, tape number three, and I'm no closer to my goal than when I started," she said. She deepened her voice, approximating a television announcer. "Previously, on Lindsey talks to herself," she giggled. "Insecurity, uncertainty, and a nagging mother. Did I forget anything?"

Keith leaned closer to the screen. He couldn't take his eyes off her.

"My future remains a giant question mark," she said, looking into the camera. "I hoped making these tapes would bring me clarity. Instead, I'm lost in the fog, if that makes any sense."

"It sure does," Keith said.

Lindsey's eyes widened. "Oh, my god," she said, looking around her. "Who said that?"

Startled by her reaction, Keith slipped out of his chair and thumped on the floor.

"Is someone there? I swear I heard you." She bent over and searched under her bed. Then she jumped up and checked the closet.

Keith climbed back into his chair and watched her through the monitor.

She closed the closet door and approached the camera, peering into the lens. "Please answer me. Who's there?"

He cleared his throat and said, "Are you talking to me?"

Her hand covered her mouth, stifling a gasp. Tears welled in her eyes. "Are you real," she whispered. "Or just in my head?"

Gooseflesh spread across his arms, and he pressed the stop button. The monitor went black. He stood and walked around the room, trying to get his head around what happened. It was impossible. Could it be a prank?

He spun in a slow circle, scanning his room.

First, he checked the back of the VCR, searching for a connection sending a signal to the unit. There wasn't.

He moved to the window, pulled back the shade, and looked outside. He expected to see someone pointing up at him and laughing, but the street was empty.

Turning back to the room he searched for a hidden camera, something recording his reactions to this preposterous concept, but he found nothing. It had to be a joke at his expense. Videotapes didn't provide two-way communication with people from the past.

But the reaction on her face when he spoke remained in his mind. *She wasn't faking it. She was as shocked and startled as I was*, he reasoned.

He returned to his chair and dropped into it, blinking rapidly and rubbing his brow.

What were other possibilities?

I might have lost my mind, he considered, but dismissed it.

He sat looking at the VCR, contemplating, thinking the best thing to do was forget it, eject the tape, power off the equipment, and go play Xbox. But he kept seeing her face, her smile, and her reaction to hearing his voice. *If she's acting, she's better than Meryl Streep.*

He pressed play again.

When the tape resumed, it showed Lindsey only inches from the lens. Her face filled the display in a blurred image. "Are you there?" she said, her voice trembling and a frightened look in her hazel eyes.

"Yes," he answered.

A slow smile spread across her face as she backed away from the camera. "You're back. What happened?" she asked with a shaky laugh. "You were in my head, and then you vanished. I wasn't sure if I imagined the whole thing. Why did you stop talking?"

"I'm sorry," Keith said. "I stopped the tape for a moment."

"Please, don't do it again," she said. "I worried I was losing my mind. I've made two tapes where I talked to myself, and it was boring as hell. But this time, I don't understand how, but your voice popped into my head. Is this happening? Are you real? What's your name? How old are you?"

"My name is Keith," he said. "I'm 22."

"I can't see you. Can you see me?"

"Sort of, but only the top half of your face."

She leaned closer to the camera, adjusting the tilt, and then leaned back, sitting on the floor, against her bed.

"Is that better?"

"Yes," he said. "Who are you?"

"My name is Lindsey. I'm 19."

"Is this a trick?" Keith asked. "Videotapes aren't supposed to do this."

"If it's a trick, it's a damn good one. Your voice is inside of me, Keith. It's as if you're right here with me. I even hear your breathing. This is the most remarkable thing I've ever experienced."

"That makes two of us."

"What made you watch my tape?"

"I found it while browsing a flea market," Keith said. "I wasn't sure what it was. But the label was so artfully decorated, and I sensed something when I held it, but I can't explain what it was. I only knew I had to watch it."

Lindsey grinned. "I'm glad you did."

"Me too."

"I have to know more about you. Do you enjoy reading?"

Keith pictured the stacks of comic books piled high against his bedroom wall. "Yeah," he said. "I love reading."

She smiled and gave him thumbs-up. "Good answer," she said. "Who's your favorite writer?"

Panic seized him. He knew reading comics didn't impress women. But he didn't want to get caught naming a writer he hadn't read. Being dishonest with her was worse than appearing childish. He scrambled for an answer. "I enjoy many writers," he said.

"But who's your favorite?" she asked, leaning closer to the camera, raising an eyebrow.

"I guess my favorite is Chris Claremont." It wasn't a lie. Claremont had written Keith's favorite *Uncanny X-Men* issues.

"Chris Claremont? I'm not familiar with that name. Male or female writer?" she asked.

"Male," he said. And before she could press him further, he asked, "Who is *your* favorite writer?"

"I love Virginia Woolf, Margaret Atwood, and right now I'm reading *The Joy Luck Club* by Amy Tan." She reached off-camera and brought the book into view. The bookmark showed she was halfway through the novel. "Books are magical, aren't they? When you read, it unlocks the potential of your imagination, transporting you anywhere, anytime. I think it's remarkable."

"Tell me more," Keith said.

"Like what?"

"It doesn't matter. I enjoy hearing you talk."

She gave the camera a curious look. "Have you seen any other of my tapes?"

"This is the first," he said.

"Where do you live?"

"New Jersey," he said. "And you?"

"California."

He glanced again at the objects on the nightstand by the bed and recognized one of them as a Walkman cassette player. "When are you recording this?" he asked.

"It's May."

"No, I mean, what year?"

"1989."

Keith shook his head in disbelief. *I wasn't even alive yet,* he thought.

"You too?" she asked.

"No," he said. "It's later than that."

Her eyes widened. *"You're from the future?"*

"Yes," he said and felt like the victim of a cruel cosmic joke.

Just my luck, he thought to himself. *I meet a remarkable young woman, and she's thirty years in the past.*

"Are there flying DeLoreans in your area?" Lindsey asked.

Keith chuckled. "God, I love those movies. But, no. Not yet."

"Movies? How far are you in the future? Is it possible for us to meet?"

His brain crunched the numbers. "Yes," he said.

"Don't tell me the year. It doesn't matter. I don't want to know. I'm thrilled for the opportunity to talk to someone who isn't me. It's nice, isn't it?"

"Absolutely," he said. "Is that your artwork hanging on the wall?"

She glanced at them, then at the camera with a blush. "Oh, damn. Ignore them. They're not very good. I'm still trying to find my style. "

"I think they're incredible. What trees are those?"

"They are Sequoia trees. Have you ever seen one in person?"

"No," Keith said.

"You *need* to correct that. Sequoias are magnificent. Nothing else on earth compares to them. The National Park is nearby, and I visit there all the time. My passion is sketching the trees and nature."

"What is this project you're doing?"

"I'll describe it next time. I'm afraid this tape will run out soon."

"How long do they last?"

"Only fifteen minutes," she said. "But I will make more so I can keep talking to you. Promise you will watch them and be there for me, okay?"

"Well, wait! How do I find them? Can you tell me where you put them?"

Someone banged on Lindsey's door, startling them both.

Keith listened as a muffled woman's voice demanded, "Who are you talking to in there, Lindsey? Is someone in there with you?" Then the banging resumed again.

Lindsey looked back at the camera and lowered her voice. "I gotta go, Keith. Find the other tapes. I'll be waiting for you." Then she reached past the lens.

Keith raised his hand to meet hers as the recording stopped and the screen switched to a display of static.

Keith dropped his hand and sighed.

"Lindsey," he whispered.

Chapter 4

Lindsey switched off the camera as the pounding on the door continued.

"Who's in there with you? Let me in, Lindsey!"

She unlocked the bedroom door, and opened it only a crack, before stumbling backward as the door flew open. Phyllis pushed past her, stormed into the room, and searched the space. She opened the closet, ruffling the clothes, and then peered under the bed.

"No one is here, Mom," Lindsey said with crossed arms and narrowed eyes.

Phyllis stood back up looking flustered. "You were talking with someone in here, and you don't have a telephone. So, where is he?"

"Why are you eavesdropping on me?" Lindsey asked. "Don't I deserve privacy?"

"I am your mother, Lindsey. I can't help but worry. And I refuse to allow you to engage in unacceptable or dangerous behavior under my roof."

"I'm almost twenty-years-old Mom. I'm not a baby anymore, stop treating me this way."

"This is my house, and these are my rules. As long as you live here, you *will* follow them. Otherwise, enter the workforce and rent an apartment. Meanwhile, I heard you, *who were you talking to?*"

"I was talking to the camera," Lindsey pointed at the tripod standing in the corner.

"Why on earth are you talking to a camera?" She stepped closer to her daughter and touched Lindsey's arm. "What is wrong with you?"

Lindsey pushed Phyllis' hand away. "Nothing is *wrong* with me. It's a video diary."

"A what?" Phyllis shook her head. "You used to be such a happy little girl," she said with a pained expression. "I remember you always laughing, singing, and playing."

"You mean before you destroyed our family?" Lindsey snarled.

Phyllis slapped her. It wasn't hard, but it stung. She clenched her teeth and said, "You will not disrespect me in my house. I won't allow it. And for your information, the decision was mutual. Your father and I *both* agreed it was for the best."

"I'm sure it was best for you. But you never gave a shit how that affected me, did you?"

Phyllis sighed. "Life is hard, and little girls can't always get what they want. It's time you understand that. The universe doesn't serve you bonbons on a silver platter. You can lock yourself in your room, and act sullen but it'll accomplish nothing, except keeping you miserable and lonely. Is that what you want?"

"Yes, mom, leave me alone. That's what I want. Is it too much to ask?"

"Well, sweetheart, *newsflash*, you aren't alone. Two other people live in this house, and you treat us with such contempt, it isn't fair. Why can't you act civil with Wit? He tries to be nice to you, and you behave as if he spat in your corn flakes."

Lindsey leaned close to her mother, locking her gaze. "He makes me uncomfortable."

"Because he tried to talk with you?"

"The way I catch him looking at me sometimes after he's been drinking. He gives me the creeps."

"Nonsense, stop being so dramatic," Phyllis said. "You imagine things. The man is trying to be a good stepfather, and you won't even meet him halfway."

Lindsey shook her head. "This is why I can't talk to you. If I try to confide in you or tell you something that's bothering me, you brush it off as nothing."

"Well, what should I say when you're talking foolishness? Wit is harmless. If you had an ounce of appreciation in you, you'd show him some gratitude. He works hard and helps us have a home and food on the table. I don't see *you* helping with that."

Lindsey threw her hands up in a sign of surrender. "Forget it," she said and headed for the door.

"Lindsey, wait," Phyllis said. "What are you doing with your life, honey? You have no friends and spend the day barricaded away and alone. And now you're carrying on conversations with a camera. That isn't normal. Stop this behavior. It's self-destructive, honey. Before you know it, you'll hear voices in your head telling you to live under a bridge."

Lindsey took a step back and furrowed her brow. "What?"

"You spend too much time alone. I think you need to socialize more. Why won't you consider going to the local college and taking those accounting classes we discussed? You'd get a secure job with that and maybe even meet some friends."

"I don't want to be an accountant, Mom, that's your idea."

"Well, what do *you* want?"

"I don't know yet!" Lindsey shouted as tears of frustration threatened to burst through.

Disgust spread across Phyllis' face. "Well get your shit together, and fast, little lady, because time is ticking. It may appear as if your entire life waits ahead of you. But trust me, one day you'll blink and realize the whole thing flew by in a flash."

Her mother stomped out of the room, slamming the door behind her.

Lindsey slumped onto the bed and finally released the emotions she had worked so hard to suppress.

Chapter 5

Keith's bike ride back to the flea market was hectic, filled with near misses and avoided collisions. He alternated between the street and the sidewalk, following the path of least resistance. As he swerved to avoid a pedestrian clutching two bags of groceries, Keith veered into the path of an oncoming car. Its horn blared, and the driver shouted obscenities out of his window, as Keith waved a partial apology. His heart raced, and legs pumped, while his focus remained fixed on reaching the flea market before Stu left for the day.

The market closed at noon on Sundays. Keith had thirty-five minutes to reach the old factory. Otherwise, he'd have to wait another week before having another chance to search for more of Lindsey's recordings.

A car door opened in front of him and he missed colliding with it by inches, twisting the handlebars and sending the bike into the middle of the road. Behind him, he heard the screech of braking tires and another angry horn blast.

At 11:45 Keith crashed into the bike rack and rushed into the market without locking up his bike.

The crowds were thin, and Keith darted around people, making a beeline for Stu's section. But as he arrived, his worst fears were realized. The area was vacant, and all the tables cleared.

"No," Keith shouted and slammed his fists down on the empty table top.

A gentle hand placed on his back startled him.

"Did you miss me that much?" Stu asked with a grin. Stacked behind him on a flatbed cart were all his sealed crates and boxes.

Keith's eyes flashed wide with excitement, and before he knew it, he hugged the old man.

"Easy there, kid, I'm a married man," Stu said and eased Keith back to a safe distance. "What did I do?"

"I was afraid you left already."

"Almost did. There wasn't much business today, and it's my daughter's birthday, so I figured I'd pack up a few minutes early."

"I have to talk to you, Stu." Keith struggled to catch his breath, his forehead slick with sweat.

"About what?"

"That tape," Keith said.

Stu's brow furrowed. "What tape, kiddo?"

"The one you gave me yesterday."

"The home movie?"

Keith nodded. "Tell me, please, is this a practical joke? I won't be mad, but I have to know."

"Practical joke? What happened?"

"I'm not sure. But watching the tape, I experienced something incredible, and I can't understand how it's possible. So I thought it might be an elaborate prank."

"It was one of those kinky sex tapes, huh? We get a few of those from time to time."

"No, no, nothing like that. Are there any more of them?"

Stu shrugged. "I don't think so. I'm not even sure how that one got in there. The box should have only had proper films and TV shows. I don't sell home movie tapes. There's no market for it."

"But it's not a home movie. It's a recording from a girl—a young woman, I mean. She said there were more tapes and I have to find them."

Stu's expression shifted to concern. "Kiddo, are you sure you're okay? You don't look too good. Are you running a fever?"

"I'm fine. Is it possible you have any more of them, Stu?"

"You're welcome to search the box again, but I doubt you'll find any in there."

Despite what Stu said, Keith turned to the cart of boxes and grabbed the one marked "VHS MOVIES." He peeled off the lid and pulled out handfuls of the tapes, piling them on the floor. As he reached the bottom, he confirmed what he already knew. It contained none of the smaller tapes.

"Shit, shit, shit."

"I'm sorry, kiddo,"

"What am I going to do, Stu," Keith said as he replaced the pile of tapes to the box.

Stu shrugged and then considered something.

"Perhaps Artie Acker," he said.

Keith looked confused. "Who?"

"*Artie Acker*. He's a vendor here too. We both get our tapes from the same distributer. I saw him on Friday when I picked up this box. He ordered one as well. Maybe he got a few of them. It's worth a shot."

Keith sealed up the box and turned to Stu. "Where can I find him?"

"He has the big set up as you enter the building, right next to the lady that sells the Beanie Babies."

Keith hugged Stu again and raced back towards the entrance, shouting to Stu, "Wish your daughter happy birthday for me!"

At 11:55, Artie Acker, dressed in a suit jacket and yellow bow tie, his thin dark hair combed over the crown of his head, packed up his displays.

Keith bumped into the table, rattling the items that remained.

"Mister Acker?" he gasped, out of breath.

"Yes," Artie said with caution.

"I need to see your VHS tapes please," Keith said.

"Sorry, son. It's closing time. Come and see me next week."

"Please, I'll pay you to look," he said, pulling a ten-dollar bill from his pocket and offering it to the vendor.

"What for?"

"Stu told me you get videotapes from the same distributor he does. Yesterday I found a tape at his table, and I want to see if you have any more of them."

Artie shrugged, snatching the cash from Keith's hands. "The green crate at the end of the table has all my VHS," he said.

Keith stumbled rushing toward it. He grabbed handfuls of the videotapes, stacking them onto the table as fast as possible.

Artie watched him with confusion. "You aren't even looking at the titles," he said.

"It's okay, I know what I'm looking for," Keith answered without looking up, pulling more tapes out, until he emptied the box. He hung his head in defeat.

"And what *are* you looking for?" Artie asked.

Keith replaced the full-sized tapes in the box. "VHS-C tapes. The kind used in camcorders."

"Oh," Artie said. "Yeah, there were a couple, but I threw them out. Nobody wants those. They shouldn't have even been in there. I'm paying for regular VHS. I bet those shysters charged me for them though."

Keith jumped up and rushed back to Artie. "Threw them where?"

"In the trash can," Artie said. "When I set up Saturday morning, I noticed them and tossed them out." Artie gestured to a blue garbage bin sitting near the entrance doors.

Keith ran to it.

"They're not in there now," Artie called after him. "Those bins get emptied every day."

Without another word, Keith sprinted outside, heading toward the bike rack. But when he reached it, he looked from one end to the other and realized his bike was missing. Someone had stolen it. He headed back to the building and ran along the perimeter. At the rear corner, he turned right and sprinted past the old truck delivery bays used when the factory operated.

His breath came in ragged gasps as he rounded the next corner of the building and found the dumpsters.

There were three of them. Giant black metal containers, seven feet high, and twenty feet long. Without hesitation, he leaped onto the side of the first bin and climbed to the top, left open so service people could toss trash bags in from the loading dock platform. Keith assessed the dumpster, half-full of black plastic garbage bags, many of them ripped open, spilling their contents of crushed soda cups, half-eaten hot dogs, dirty napkins, tissues, and other debris, onto the bags below them.

"Thank god it isn't summer," Keith said and jumped inside.

His approach was systematic, tossing each sealed trash bag out of the dumpster and into the parking lot until only ripped ones remained. Keith reasoned the trash from Saturday should be at the top of the pile, so he'd search those first and dig deeper into the heap if he found nothing.

The work made him nauseous. Despite the chilly October air, the festering stench of old garbage inside the bin caused him to gag. His hands coated with a sticky combination of flat soda, wet paper, and other things he tried not to identify. His shoes and socks soaked through and he felt the skin of his feet and toes pruning in the damp nastiness that covered them.

With over sixty bags tossed outside the dumpster, he searched the contents of the remaining ripped ones. Each time his hands encountered something vile, he fought back the urge to retch.

He tried to look past the trash surrounding him and focus on Lindsey. If he could get through this, the reward was more time with her, another conversation. The technique worked. The soggy piles of refuse became invisible to him. He pictured her smile, and the tear she shed when she said she could hear him.

He was dripping wet with the stench of trash when he climbed from the dumpster, empty-handed.

A pile of trash bags awaited him on the pavement, outside the dumpster. One by one he tore them open digging through the fetid contents. The variety of garbage filling the bags surprised him. Broken vinyl records, shattered antique plates, waterlogged dolls, old radios, portable televisions, ripped clothing, and lots of half-eaten food and unfinished beverages.

He worked through half the bags when an angry voice shouted to him from the loading platform.

"What the hell are you doing there, buddy?"

Keith looked up from the bag he was sifting through and saw a janitor looking at him with a reaction of confusion and repulsion.

"I threw something in the trash here on Saturday by mistake, and I'm trying to find it," Keith said.

"Saturday?" the janitor responded. "Then you are looking in the wrong dumpster." He pointed to the second dumpster. "That has the trash from yesterday."

Keith darted toward the other dumpster but stopped as the janitor shouted at him.

"Hey, where the hell do you think you're going? Clean that shit up, or I'll come down there and kick your skinny ass."

It took Keith another hour to pick up the scattered garbage he had tossed out of the first dumpster and begin his search through the second one.

He'd skipped breakfast that morning and missed lunch too. But despite being weak with hunger, he couldn't even consider eating. The overpowering reek of refuse made the idea repulsive. He continued the quest.

Bag after bag he searched, with the fading autumn sunlight now making it hard to see. His willpower diminished, and he ached from hours of hunching over in a sea of trash. Doubt took hold of him.

What the hell am I doing? This is ridiculous.

He pushed back against the nagging voice in his head and tore open another bag.

And there it was.

Sitting atop a pile of dirty paper plates was a VHS-C tape marked *Tape #4* and surrounded by an intricate, illustrated border. His hand moved to cover his gaping mouth, but the stench made him retch, and he moved it away, snatching the tape and holding it up against the fading light of an October sky.

Elated, he exited the dumpster when he remembered what Artie said to him.

"There were a couple in the box, but I threw them out."

Keith dove back into the open bag, digging deeper inside, ignoring the things squishing against his fingers as he searched. At the bottom of the bag, he found two more: *Tape #5* and *Tape #6.*

"Yes!" he shouted, his voice reverberating inside the metal box.

He pushed them into his pocket and completed the search of the bag, confirming no other tapes remained inside. Then he clenched his eyes and collapsed against the wall of the dumpster. Tears of joy squeezed out between his closed lids. Part of it came from sheer exhaustion and the relief of completing the awful task. But the main reason was the realization he'd get to see her again.

Chapter 6

The walk home from the flea market was brutal. Darkness had fallen, leaving the autumn air chilled and bitter. Keith tried to hail a taxi and got one to stop, despite his appearance. But the moment he opened the back door and tried to climb into the car, the driver got a whiff of him and waved his arms in protest.

"No fucking way," he shouted, gesturing for Keith to back away. "You smell very bad. You will ruin my cab," he said. "Get out!"

"But it's fourteen blocks to my apartment," Keith said.

"Not my problem," the driver sped off, with the door slamming closed.

With muscles aching and soaked to the bone in sweat and dumpster juice, Keith started the long slog home.

He was sure moisture had seeped into the tapes from the liquids inside the trash bags. If he tried to play them in that condition, the videotape would bind up in the machine, damaging or destroying the tapes. He couldn't let that happen. They needed to dry out before being viewed. From his experience dropping mobile phones into toilets, Keith knew the most efficient way to extract the moisture from an item was to seal it in a bag of uncooked rice.

He began to think about how to find the other tapes. The first two recordings were missing, along with any Lindsey made after *Tape #6*. He needed to locate the name of the company where Stu and Artie bought their videotapes, and contact them to determine if they had any others.

But the one thing he wanted to do at that moment was to peel off his reeking clothes, gather them into a pile, soak them in kerosene and set them ablaze. He was confident only fire could remove the odor wafting off of them.

Then he would take a long, hot shower, scrubbing his skin red, until he washed away every remnant of his dumpster dive.

Thirty minutes later he arrived at his apartment building, with every muscle in his body groaning in agony. With the elevator being serviced, he needed to climb the stairs to the second floor. Exhaustion took over, and he almost collapsed on the top step as his weak legs wobbled and gave out. He grabbed the railing with both hands and prevented himself from plummeting down the cement stairs to the landing.

With a deep breath, he summoned his final ounce of strength and pulled himself up to the stairwell exit. He opened it and fell into the hall. From there he crawled to his apartment door. If anyone in the building had seen his reeking form writhing on the floor, they would have called the cops.

From his knees, he fished his keys out and dropped a tape on the hallway carpet. He snatched it back, holding it close to his chest, as he fumbled to unlock the door.

He crept into his apartment and collapsed passed out in a stinking heap on the floor.

●

Keith's dreams were a crazy jumble of the last two days. He saw Stu and Artie laughing at him as he swam in an ocean of garbage. The janitor from the flea market was there too.

"He's swimming in the wrong ocean," the janitor said, and all three of them howled with laughter. To escape their ridicule, he dove beneath the surface, kicking his legs, propelling himself away from them. The trash water changed to a bright, cerulean blue sea, with waves cresting above his head and crashing into foam.

He stopped when he reached a small desert island. A lone palm tree offered the only shade. Keith crawled from the water and collapsed beneath the tree.

He closed his eyes and whispered, "I'm alone. I'm alone."

Then he heard a voice in his head. It was Lindsey.

"Use your imagination," she said. "And everything is possible."

In the dream he opened his eyes and saw her sitting beside him, reading an X-Men comic book.

"It's not as good as Virginia Woolf," she said. "But I like it."

Keith felt his heart swell, watching the sunlight dance in her long dark hair, flowing in the breeze. She smiled at him.

"Kiss me," she whispered and leaned into him, closing her eyes and parting her full lips. Then she halted. "You smell very bad," she said. "You will ruin my cab."

Keith's eyes flew open, scattering the dream.

A quick glance at the clock showed he'd slept for twelve hours on the floor of his apartment and was late for work. He took a deep breath, then fell into a coughing fit, gaging on the odor still wafting off of him. He jumped up and peeled off the festering clothes.

Naked, his whole body pruned from sleeping in damp, trash-soaked garments, he grabbed the tapes from his coat pocket and rushed into his kitchen to find the box of rice. He poured the contents into a storage bag, dropped the three recordings inside and sealed it.

Next, he sprinted to the bathroom, jumping into the shower he spun the knobs on, blasting himself in a cascade of ice-cold water. He shivered as he scrubbed his wrinkled skin and shampooed his hair in minutes. Just as the warm water arrived, he leaped out of the shower and toweled dry.

He shook four ibuprofen tablets into his hand and dry-swallowed them.

In his bedroom, he pulled on a clean shirt and pants, socks and shoes, and hurried out the door. Outside the apartment, he flagged a taxi and gave the driver the address for his job, then collapsed back in the seat rubbing his aching head.

He worked for a small manufacturing firm on the outskirts of Hoboken, called Blair, Inc. They built and assembled vacuum cleaner attachments. It occupied a single-floor brick structure in a small industrial park on the edge of the city. The offices, at the front of the building, filled a third of the available space, while the machine shop at the back took the rest. Four desks and a receptionist counter filled the cramped office, illuminated by buzzing fluorescent lights suspended from the water-stained ceiling. Three of the workspaces were for salespeople. The fourth was Keith's. His job involved coordinating between the sales and manufacturing departments.

His boss, a short, balding, man, with a sour disposition, stood beside the receptionist, with her phone receiver to his ear, when Keith entered.

"Hi, Mr. Witlicki," Keith said with a sheepish wave. "Sorry, I'm late."

"Guess I can stop calling you now," Witlicki said, returning the receiver to the cradle and shaking his head. "Where have you been?"

"Someone stole my bike," Keith said.

"And you took an hour to find a taxi?" he asked.

"Well, part of that I spent looking for the bike, sorry."

Witlicki sighed. "Manufacturing is waiting on today's orders. I tried to locate them on your workspace, but it was a cluttered mess, I stopped. I've seen nothing so disorganized in my life. How do you find things?" He gestured to Keith's desk. It was smothered with invoices, catalogs, notes, and folders. "The whole department is waiting for them, Nolan."

"I'll get them," Keith said, hurrying to his desk and sifting through the pile.

"They've been waiting over an hour."

"Yes, sir."

Keith shuffled through the mess, and located the folder, holding it up triumphantly. "Found them," he said with a smile.

"Gee, I don't know how I didn't see them," his boss said. "Deliver that to manufacturing. Then I want to see you in my office."

Keith headed to the manufacturing room, through a pair of heavy metal doors. He handed the day's order sheets to the foreman and apologized for his lateness. The foreman laughed. "Doesn't bother me," he said. "Now we all get an hour of overtime."

But instead of heading back to the office and having his boss explain it again, Keith found an open computer terminal and clicked on the browser link, typing a search for *VHS tape distributors in Hoboken*. It generated only one result.

He dialed the phone number on his cell.

"Multi-Media Wholesale," said a woman's voice. "How can I help you?"

"Hello," Keith said, lowering his tone to keep the conversation away from any prying coworkers. "I need to talk to someone regarding videotapes distributed by your company."

"Hold a moment please," said the woman.

While he waited, a salesperson from the front office entered the manufacturing floor and waved at Keith. "The little prick is waiting for you," he said.

Keith nodded. "I'll be right there."

On the phone, a male voice answered. "This is Tom," he said.

"Yes, hello. Um, I discovered four home movie videotapes last week in boxes of VHS tapes sold by you. I need to know if you have any more in your possession."

"No," the man said.

"Well, how can you answer without the details," Keith asked.

"I don't need any details. We keep no inventory here. The only stock we distribute is what people have ordered."

"Where were the tapes ordered from?"

"Our VHS tapes come from a distributor in Ohio."

"Can I have their name?" Keith asked.

"Why are you asking?"

"It involves... a missing person," Keith said, improvising.

"Oh," the man said. "They're called Duncan Distributors."

Keith jotted the name on a piece of scrap paper beside the computer. "Thank you for your time."

He ended the call and did an Internet search for Duncan Distributors. He found the phone number and dialed it. After three rings, a young-sounding woman answered.

"Thank you for calling Duncan. This is Tracy, how may I direct your call?"

"Hi," Keith said, "I need to speak to someone in your warehouse regarding VHS tapes you shipped to Multi-Media Wholesale in Hoboken, New Jersey."

"Sorry, Rory handles home video. He's not in today. If you leave me your name and number, he'll get back to you tomorrow," she said.

Keith gave her his info and disconnected.

●

Mr. Witlicki's office was tucked in the corner of the building's front room. The location afforded him an unobstructed view of the office, and a full window overlooking the parking lot. Keith entered and closed the door. On the dark, wood-paneled walls hung various framed certificates including one from the Chamber of Commerce, several customer service awards, and a diploma from Rutgers University.

Witlicki sat behind a metal desk, leaning back with his bulbous belly protruding above his belt buckle. His eyes narrowed as Keith faced him.

"What took you so long?"

"I wanted to be sure there weren't any questions about the orders."

"Sit down, Mr. Nolan," Witlicki said.

Keith sat in a metal folding chair opposite the desk.

"Is there something wrong, Mr. Nolan? Do you have a problem that prevents you from getting to work on time?"

"No," Keith responded.

"Yet it happens several times a month."

"I've been reliable lately, for the most part."

"Are you happy with this job, Mr. Nolan?"

Keith hesitated a moment. "Well, yes," he said.

"Is that so?" Witlicki asked, leaning forward and placing his arms on the desktop. "Then explain why your workspace is a cluttered mess, you're often late, and your attitude appears..." he paused, searching for the word. "Disinterested," he said after a moment. "Is there someplace else you'd rather be? Not everyone is cut out for the high-pressure world of vacuum accessories."

"No, Mr. Witlicki, I like my job very much," Keith said.

"Evidence suggests the contrary. I gave you this job as a favor to Professor DiMeo at Rutgers, because I'm an alumnus, too," he said, gesturing to his diploma. "Somehow you impressed her. She said you possessed great potential, but I'll be honest, I don't see it. Don't make me regret providing you this opportunity. I suggest you show improvement, Mr. Nolan, post-haste. Treat your job with the respect it deserves and stop being late. This is our busy time. We need all hands on deck, yes?"

Keith nodded.

"Are you part of this crew?"

"Yes, sir."

"Then act that way. And you don't leave tonight until everything clears shipping, understood?"

"Yes."

"Good. Now go clean up your desk."

Keith stood and stepped toward the door.

"One last thing, Nolan. Work on your hygiene. You smell like you slept in a trash can."

Chapter 7

After hearing Keith's voice in her head for the first time, Lindsey questioned her sanity. She realized the experience was impossible. *Maybe it will stop,* she wondered, but the mere thought of that upset her. She didn't want it to go away she needed it to continue.

She tried several times to summon Keith without the video camera, to call to him in her mind. The first time was in the shower, feeling the warm caress of hot water running down her body, steam rising around her. She closed her eyes and whispered, "Are you with me, Keith?" Desperate for him to respond, she waited but heard nothing but the streaming water.

Another try happened in her bed, as Lindsey hoped his voice, soft and soothing, could speak to her as she surrendered to sleep. To slip into dreams with him in her head, keeping her company, sharing her secrets, was the only thing she wanted. But her efforts failed. Instead of Keith's dulcet tone, she got the monotonous drone of the television set coming from her mother's bedroom. For whatever reason, her conversation with Keith happened only while the video camera was on and a tape was rolling. So she planned what she'd include in the next recording, but it required a road trip first.

Her destination was the town library to locate books by Keith's favorite writer, Chris Claremont. Lindsey prided herself on being well-read, but the work of this writer had eluded her.

The anticipation of correcting that, along with the promise of discussing it with Keith, had her giddy.

She pulled into the library parking lot and exited the car, gazing up at a cobalt sky filled with white clouds and bright sunshine. A warm breeze embraced her, whispering through the branches of Valley Oak trees surrounding the building.

Inside the library, a line of people waited for the librarian—mothers with young children clutching picture books, and elderly folks carrying novels by Robert Ludlum, Judith Krantz, and Sidney Sheldon. Lindsey savored it. She embraced every visit to the library as an invitation to adventure. It was where her joy of reading blossomed.

She walked past the check-out counter and made her way to the card catalog, a massive rack of dark wood drawers, filled with thousands of cards representing the entire contents of the library, organized by author, book title, and subject matter.

As she pulled out the drawer containing listings CLA-CLO, she flipped through the cards, searching for something from author Chris Claremont, but found no listing. She tried different spellings, but it turned up nothing. She wondered if he was a writer from the future and perhaps his books hadn't been written yet. She closed the drawer and headed to the librarian's desk.

The line of people had dwindled, and she approached the librarian, a tall, thin woman with curly red hair and emerald eyes.

"Hello," Lindsey said. "Can you help me? I am having trouble finding a writer in the catalog."

Behind her, a short, middle-aged man with thinning hair got in line, holding a stack of Elmore Leonard novels.

"Who is the writer?" the librarian asked.

"His name is Chris Claremont," Lindsey said.

"And you checked his name alphabetically?"

"Yes," said Lindsey.

The man behind her asked, "Are you an X-Men fan?"

Lindsey turned around with a furrowed brow. "I'm sorry?"

"X-Men," the man repeated. "You mentioned Chris Claremont, right? He's a writer of X-Men."

"He is?" said Lindsey, confused. "I'm sorry, who are the X-Men?"

"It's a comic book series published by Marvel Comics. But you won't find them here, despite my best efforts." He gave a disapproving look to the librarian. "The library doesn't consider them proper literature."

"*Comic books?*" Lindsey asked.

"Yeah. I read them when I was a kid, back in the 60s. The early stuff was goofy. But the stories now are fantastic, and Claremont is the main writer. His *Days of Future Past* was exceptional," the man said.

"Where could I read them?"

"Until they stock them here," he said, with another scowl toward the librarian, "You need to go to a comic book store."

"Is there one nearby?"

"Sure, in Tulare, it's not far. They have a great selection."

"Could you give me directions?"

"Sure," he said.

Lindsey opened her purse, pulling out a scrap piece of paper and a pen, and jotted down the route. "And what was the name of the story you mentioned?"

"*Days of Future Past*. Issues #141 and #142 of *Uncanny X-Men*. It's one of my favorites. The story takes place in both the present and the future."

"That sounds familiar," Lindsey said, scribbling the details. "Thank you very much."

"No problem, always happy to help a fellow comic fan. Hope you enjoy 'em. Claremont's a genius."

"I'm sure I will." Lindsey shook the man's hand and hurried out of the library.

She found the comic book store, *Superheroes' Dungeon*, in a strip mall on Route 137, between a gourmet coffee shop and a laundromat. Across the front windows were posters of characters rendered in bright colors of blue, red and yellow. Most of them Lindsey didn't recognize, but one she did, Spider-man, featured near the front door, hanging upside down from the top of the Empire State Building, reading a comic book.

As Lindsey walked into the shop, she was greeted by the welcoming aroma of aged paper. She had always found the smell of old books a near aphrodisiac, but she hadn't expected to experience it in a comic book store.

The long wall running to the back of the shop overflowed with thousands of comics stacked into cubbyholes. Lindsey knew there were hundreds of superheroes but didn't realize the art form had also expanded far beyond that. There were books featuring romance, adventure, history and science fiction. She found the variety stunning.

On one of the display cases beneath a sign proclaiming TOP RECOMMENDATION, Lindsey saw a book called *Maus* by Art Spiegelman. It was a graphic novel of a Holocaust survivor from Nazi Germany, but it used cats and mice as the main characters. The cover depicted a striking image of cowering mice, clinging to each other while a cat rendered as Hitler, loomed behind them within a swastika.

"That's a powerful book," said a voice behind her, startling Lindsey.

She turned to see a man walking toward her from the back of the store, his arms filled with boxes of more books. He was a big man with a trim, salt and pepper beard and wore an L.A. Dodger's baseball cap.

"I thought comics were goofy fun for kids," Lindsey said.

"They started out that way, sure. But as readers got older, the stories became more adult. Now, they restrict certain titles to mature readers only." He set the boxes on the counter. "And that book," he said, pointing to *Maus*, "will change the way people think about comic books. It got nominated for the National Book Critics Circle."

"Wow," Lindsey said.

"I'm Dan," he said and flashed an infectious smile. "Is that the book you wanted?"

"No," Lindsey said, fishing the crumpled note out of her purse. "I was hoping to find books by Chris Claremont."

"Funny, you don't resemble the typical X-Men fan," he said. "Are you looking for a particular issue?"

"*Days of Future Past*," she said without hesitation.

"Man, I love that one. Let me see if I have any in stock."

Dan walked back the way he came and stopped at a table covered in long white boxes. Printed on the front of each one was the name of a comic book title. He moved to the last row and flipped through the books.

"Let's see," he said. "122, 128, 134, 139. Ah, here they are, issues 141 and 142." He removed them from the box with great care.

Lindsey noticed they had clear plastic sleeves protective them.

"Are these issues for you, or are they a gift for someone special?"

"They're for me," she said. "A friend recommended the writer."

Dan carried the books back to the front of the shop.

"Are you familiar with the series?"

Lindsey shook her head.

"The X-Men are mutants," he said. "They've developed special abilities, different from normal people, and the rest of the world sees them as a threat. The mutants are outcasts."

Under her breath, she said, "Aren't we all."

He handed the books to Lindsey. The covers featured dynamic artwork and bright colors. The second book proclaimed in bold, stark letters: *This Issue: EVERYBODY DIES!*

"That's a spoiler, isn't it?"

Dan smiled. "More of a teaser, I'd say."

"Is this the final issue?" she asked.

"No way," Dan said with a laugh.

"Can you clue me on the story?"

"It spans two time periods, the present, and a dark future in the year 2013, with giant, killer robots created to destroy the mutants."

"Oh," she said and nodded.

"Can I get you any other titles?"

"No, that should do it for now," she said reaching for her purse.

Dan stepped behind the register and rang up her purchase.

"That will be $17.03," he said and smiled.

Lindsey stared at him a moment. "Is there a mistake?" she asked.

"What do you mean?"

"The covers say the books are fifty cents each."

"That was the price when they first published, several years ago. But these are back issues now, and in-demand, increasing their value. Also, these two are in near-mint condition, no creases or tears on the cover. I might have them in a lower quality. Those issues would be cheaper. Do you want me to check?"

"No, that's okay," Lindsey said, replacing the two dollar bills she expected to pay with, and took out a twenty instead, handing it to Dan.

He gave her the change and placed the books with care into a brown paper bag.

"Treat them well. Their value should continue to increase. So try not to damage the covers or pages when you read them. Does your friend shop here, too?"

"No," she said. "He lives in New Jersey."

"Well, if he ever visits, bring him by."

"I'll do that. Thanks, Dan," she said. "Nice meeting you."

Chapter 8

Hoboken, New Jersey
October 23, 2019, 6:35 PM

After making up the missed hour at work, Keith confirmed all the orders had shipped, and returned home in the bitter chill of night, numb and almost as exhausted as the day before.

Once inside his apartment he stripped off his work clothes and climbed into the shower, giving himself the proper cleaning he'd missed that morning. He soaped up his body while his mind focused on Lindsey.

She had pervaded his thoughts the entire day, with his emotions riding a roller coaster. In one moment he felt elated, knowing he had three more tapes to watch, which meant 45-minutes of time to spend with her, talking, laughing and learning every detail regarding her. But then his mood crashed with the realization that unless he found more of her recordings, those 45-minutes represented the time he had remaining with her.

After the shower, he toweled dry and slipped into a long-sleeve t-shirt, featuring a snarling image of Wolverine, his favorite of the X-Men, and sweatpants.

In the kitchen, he pulled the tapes out of the bag of rice and felt the tingling sensation, like static electricity, in his fingertips as he touched them. He brought the cassettes over to the equipment rack. *Tape #4* was the next to watch. Its label had a different border than the intricate latticework around the edge of *Tape #3*. This one featured tiny, multi-colored hearts.

His face beamed with a big, goofy grin as he loaded the tape into the adapter he hoped the rice had done its job. As he slid the cassette into the VCR, he whispered a silent prayer that the tape wouldn't jam. Pressing play he heard the whirring of the gears and motors as the tape threaded through the playback assembly. Then the monitor flashed, and Lindsey's bedroom appeared. Keith heaved a sigh of relief.

Lindsey stepped out from behind the camera and sat cross-legged on the floor of her bedroom, close to the lens.

"Keith?" she said. "Are you there?"

"Yes I am," Keith said with a sense of relief and watched her face light up.

"They say people who hear voices in their head are crazy. Do I look crazy to you?"

"No, you look beautiful," he said and smiled as she blushed.

"Hey," she said. "This isn't fair. You can see me, but I can't see you. Describe yourself."

Keith thought for a moment. "Do you know who Brad Pitt is?" he asked.

"No," she said.

"Too bad, cause we could be twins," he lied.

"Really?"

"Oh, yeah. Chiseled chin and rock-hard abs."

"So you're a statue?" she teased.

Keith laughed. "I am just an ordinary guy. Nothing special."

"Well, help me picture you. How tall are you?"

"Five-ten."

"What color hair and eyes?"

"My hair is like a sandy blond, cut short. My eyes are brown. I wear glasses for reading."

"Mmm, sounds kinda hunky."

Keith laughed nervously.

"Well, speaking of reading," she said. "I finished *The Joy Luck Club* and needed to find something new to read." She reached off camera, biting her lower lip, and pulled back the copies of the comics.

"Holy shit!"

She laughed. "Did I surprise you?"

"That is so awesome," he said. "I can't believe you bought an X-Men comic."

"Not one," she said in a teasing tone. "Two!" She revealed the second issue to Keith.

"That's one of my favorite stories."

"The parallels of a story spanning present and future were an interesting coincidence," she said.

"You read it?"

"Of course," she said, "I had to read a story by your favorite writer."

"And?"

"It was tricky understanding who everyone was, and what their powers were. But I enjoyed it," she said.

"On Saturday I bought issue #117 of Uncanny X-Men. It was the final comic needed to complete my collection."

"How much did it cost?"

"Don't ask," he said, with a chuckle.

"Tell me. Should I keep these copies in their *'near-mint'* condition?"

"I paid over two-hundred dollars for it."

"Oh my god," she gasped. "Dan was right."

"Who's Dan?" Keith asked, with a tinge of jealousy.

"The comic shop guy."

Keith relaxed. "I've been collecting X-Men books since I was a kid. My dad bought me my first issues for my tenth birthday and then gave me his childhood collection. It took twelve years to finish the run, but I think he'd be proud."

"Did you tell him?" she asked.

Keith sighed. "Um..." He stopped for a moment, to keep control of his emotions. "When I was fourteen, my parents were in a car crash," he said. "After that, my aunt raised me."

"Oh, Keith, I'm sorry," Lindsey said, holding her hands in front of her mouth.

"That was eight years ago, and I still miss them, you know? But I'm okay. Are you close with your mom and dad?"

Lindsey shook her head. "My parents divorced when I was sixteen," she said. "We were living in Hawaii. My dad is still there. I haven't seen him in three years. My mom moved us to California and married the first guy she met here."

"Is he nice?" Keith asked.

Lindsey didn't answer. She leaned past the lens, checking the camera's display. "Our tape is running out. We don't have much time left. I don't want to waste any on them."

"Sorry," Keith said, realizing he'd touched a nerve.

She waved it away. "It's okay. You're what I'm interested in, tell me more. Do you have a job?"

"I work for a manufacturing company here in Hoboken."

"That sounds impressive," she said. "Is it fun?"

Keith shrugged. "Nah, but I have to pay the bills, right?"

Lindsey laughed. "I guess. I'm trying to figure that out, too."

"Tell me more about your art," Keith said.

Lindsey laughed and shrugged. "Not much to tell. My art keeps me sane." She chuckled and shrugged. "But can a girl who hears a boy talking in her head be sane?"

She stood and removed one of her sketches of the Sequoias from the wall. As she sat back down, she showed it to the camera. "You told me last time you want to see these trees, remember?"

"Yeah," he said.

"Maybe I can help you with that," Lindsey said and smiled.

"I found three more of your tapes in a dumpster. This one and two others," Keith said. "I'm trying to find more, but..."

"What?" she asked. "You dug through a dumpster to find my tapes?"

"Yeah," Keith mumbled.

Lindsey leaned in, her eyes widening. "That may be the most romantic thing anyone has ever done for me," she said.

"You might not have felt that way if you got a whiff of me afterward," Keith said, and Lindsey laughed.

"I located where the tapes first shipped from. It's a place in Ohio. I called and left a message. They're supposed to call me tomorrow. But I'm worried what happens if they can't help me."

"I'll keep making them, I promise. You'll find more," Lindsey said.

"Maybe you could put the tapes somewhere safe and then tell me where to find them."

Lindsey considered that. "But if I did that, how would you have found the first one? I think we need to trust in the power of fate. It hasn't let us down yet."

"I hope you're right. I love talking to you," Keith said. "You're smart, funny, crazy talented, *and* you read comics. You are one in a million, Lindsey."

Tears welled in her eyes. "I love talking to you too, Keith." She touched her fingers to the lens of the camera.

Keith raised his hand and touched the monitor. "Are you okay?"

She laughed and wiped at her eyes. "Talk to you soon," she said. "The next tape has a big surprise for you."

His mind raced as a big, goofy grin spread across his face.

She blew him a kiss, and the screen went to snow.

Keith sat for several minutes debating if he should pop in the next tape. He craved it, ached for it, but he knew only two more videotapes remained and chose to wait.

His thoughts shifted to trying to understand what was happening to them. The experience defied logic. Was it magic, or might he be misunderstanding the technology?

He opened his laptop, navigated to the browser and typed in a search for *VCR repair*. He found a listing for a shop in his neighborhood and dialed the phone number.

The line rang four times without being answered. Keith pulled the phone from his ear, preparing to hang up when someone answered.

"Rocky's Repairs," said a gravelly male voice.

"Hi," Keith said. "Um, do you guys work on VCR's?"

"Yup."

"Could I bring my unit in?"

"I'm closing up in about an hour."

"I'm only around the corner from you," Keith said.

"What's the problem you're having with it?"

"It would be easier to explain in person."

"I'll check it out, but if it needs work, you'll have to leave it," the man said.

"I understand," Keith said. "See you soon."

Chapter 9

With his backpack strapped to his shoulders, Keith located Rocky's Repair Shop in the basement of an old brownstone just a few blocks from his apartment. From the sidewalk, he spotted the sign, weathered and faded, waving in the autumn breeze. It was illuminated by a flickering fluorescent bulb while thick iron bars protected the windows. Keith descended the cracked cement steps and opened the heavy door, decorated with decals for parts and equipment companies. A tiny bell suspended from the top of the door jingled, announcing his arrival.

As he stepped in, stale air, dense with dust, cigarette smoke, and cleaning chemicals assaulted his lungs. Stacked equipment cluttered the cramped space. Piles of stereos, radios, record players, TV's, VCR's, and movie projectors littered the place. An old work mat, stained and tattered, covered the countertop, advertising the 1978 Bell & Howell line of film projectors. Scattered around were various tools—screwdrivers, sockets, pliers, and a can of WD-40.

From behind a wall of boxes, a man emerged. He had a cigarette clenched between his lips. His hair was a curly mess of gray, and he wore glasses with a thin wire frame balanced on the tip of his nose. He looked at Keith over the top of them.

"Can I help you?"

"Are you, Rocky?" Keith asked. "I called a little while ago about my VCR."

"Yup," Rocky said, and walked behind the counter, opposite Keith. "What's the problem?"

"You've probably been working on these things a long time, right?"

He nodded.

"Have you ever heard of someone having a strange experience while watching a tape?"

"A woman in Newport had a heart attack while watching *The Exorcist*."

"That's not what I mean." Keith pulled the straps of his backpack off his shoulders, unzipped it, and removed the deck, placing it on the counter. "I'm not well educated on VCR's. I use mine to watch anime, most of the time. But I was wondering if the technology allowed, um, two-way communication."

Rocky's brow furrowed. "Come again?"

"If someone recorded a tape a long time ago, with a video camera, can you talk to them, through the tape?"

Rocky's eyes narrowed. "Son, what is your major malfunction?"

"I don't understand," Keith said.

"That's clear," Rocky said with a laugh which led to a bout of coughing. He pulled the remains of the cigarette from his mouth and crushed it into an ashtray shaped like a miniature record player. He placed a hand on top of the VCR. "You think there's a flux capacitor in there that lets you travel to the past? Whatever you're smokin', I'd like some."

"So that isn't possible?" Keith asked.

"Are you pulling my leg?"

"No. I found a tape, and when I played it, the person—this girl—she responded to my questions. We talked to each other. And I wasn't sure how that was possible."

"It isn't," Rocky said. "Period. End of the sentence. The tape is magnetic. The unit records image and sound sent from a source, either a camera or television signal. Whatever gets recorded stays that way. You can't communicate. It's not a damn telephone."

He grabbed the power cable from the VCR, plugged into an outlet below the counter and connected a coax cable to the output connector at the back of the unit. He picked up a remote control and pressed the power button. The television mounted on the wall illuminated a blue screen. From a shelf on the wall beside the counter, he pulled out a VHS tape labeled *TEST TAPE*, loaded it into the machine, and pressed play.

The monitor on the wall flickered to life, and an episode of the television show *Taxi* displayed, showing a scene between Danny DeVito and Tony Danza. Rocky bent down in front of the VCR, pushed open the flap and shouted into it, "CAN YOU GUYS HEAR ME?" On the screen, DeVito and Danza continued their conversation uninterrupted. "HELLLLOOOOOO?" Rocky bellowed. No response.

Standing up, Rocky gestured to Keith. "Do you want to see if it works for you?"

Embarrassed, Keith shook his head. "Sorry to waste your time," he said.

"If videotapes are talking to you, kid, maybe you should seek the help of a medical professional, instead of an electronics technician."

He ejected the tape, disconnected the cables and handed the VCR back to Keith.

"Thanks," Keith said, sliding the deck back into his backpack and headed for the exit.

"Kid?" Rocky called after him. "You're serious about this? You ain't just yankin' my chain?"

Keith turned back. "I am serious," he said. "It happened."

"When you play the tape again, do you have a *different* conversation, or does it stay the same?"

Keith shrugged. "I've only watched them once."

"The contents of that tape *CAN NOT CHANGE*," Rocky said. "If you play the tape again, seeing and hearing different things than the first time you watched it, you are hallucinating, son. But if someone made a tape, knowing how you would respond to certain questions, then I guess that *is* possible. But when you play the tape again, the questions and responses should be exactly same. You understand what I mean?"

Keith nodded. "Thanks, Rocky," he said.

Rocky pulled a fresh cigarette out of a pack and lit it up. A halo of gray-blue smoke encircled his head, "No problem. Now get outta here."

Chapter 10

Visalia, California
May 8, 1989, 3:29 PM

Lindsey walked out the back door of the house, into the warm, welcoming spring air, surrounded by the scents and colors of rejuvenated life: blooming flowers in her mother's garden, the green leaves of the sycamore trees, and the aroma of fresh-cut grass.

She stepped off the back porch, and closed her eyes, enjoying the comforting beams of sunshine on her face. It felt like being recharged by glowing energy, soothing, calming, and divine.

"Are you meditating?" Wit laughed.

His voice shattered the illusion. He stepped out of the one-car garage that sat at the end of the driveway. Lindsey saw her mother's car parked inside with the hood raised. A large metal pan below it on the cement floor caught draining fluid. Wit, dressed in faded, dirty coveralls, stained with streaks of grease and motor oil, wiped his hands with a rag, his fingertips blackened with road dirt. He cocked his head to the side as if unsure what to make of her.

"You sure are an odd one, Lindsey," he said.

"What do you want, Wit?" she asked.

As he stepped out of the shade of the garage into the sunlight, his scalp shined through his thinning hair. "I want to talk to you a minute," he said. "Is that a problem?"

"I have to be somewhere," Lindsey said, turning to walk to her car.

"Wanna go camping this weekend?" he asked.

Lindsey stopped and turned back to him, her brow furrowed. "Are you joking?"

"I'm aware of your fondness for the National Park. Might be nice to pitch a tent and commune with nature for a few days. Whattya say?"

"Mom *hates* camping," Lindsey said. "You should know that."

Wit shrugged. "Well, if she's not interested, the two of us can go."

"Are you high?" she asked. "I'm not going camping with you, Wit."

"Cut me some slack. I'm just trying to connect with you, Lindsey. We should be friends. You think we have nothing in common, but I love the outdoors too—fishing, hiking, *and* camping. I know that park is your favorite place. I think it'd be nice."

"Not going to happen," Lindsey said, dismissing the topic, and turning again to leave.

"Hang on," he said. "I want to talk to you about your mom."

"What?" Lindsey asked, annoyed.

"Why do you constantly gotta rile her up?"

"I don't do that."

Wit's face expanded into that hideous grin again, showing his yellowed, crooked teeth.

"Oh, I think you do," he said. "No matter what that woman says, you gotta give her grief."

Lindsey shifted her weight from one leg to the other, crossing her arms over her chest.

"She worries about you, and you treat her like shit," Wit said, the smile had vanished. "*That* becomes a problem for me, you understand?"

"No," Lindsey said.

"Your mother is a very uptight woman. She gets rattled easy. But no one sets her off more than you. When she's uptight and bitchy, she takes it out on me. I want to help her relax, calm down, make her feel good, you understand? The way a husband and wife should. But I can't do that if she's all jacked-up, because of you."

For a moment, Lindsey looked at him trying to process his words.

"Are you saying my relationship with my mother is messing up your sex life, Wit?"

Wit laughed, but it held no humor. "That's one way to put it."

"Tough shit," Lindsey said and turned to her car.

Wit grabbed her by the elbow. The contact was unexpected and startled her. He stepped closer to her. His scent, a blend of sweat and engine oil, pervaded.

"You got a real mouth on you, buttercup," he said, dropping his voice to a conspiratorial level. "And if you ain't careful, it may get you in real trouble one day."

She yanked away from his grip. "Keep your god-damned hands off me," she hissed.

He flashed a hideous grin. "You got spunk, girl. I like that. Remember what I said about your mama. Stop being an uptight bitch."

"Fuck you," she said, and stormed off to her car, her face flushed with anger. She opened the driver's door, entered her vehicle and slammed the door closed as hard as she could, battling the urge to scream in rage.

Wit stood at the end of the driveway, wiping his hands and staring at her, still wearing that awful smile.

Chapter 11

Keith expected his visit to the technician would result in embarrassment, and it did. But it confirmed his connection with Lindsey had nothing to do with his equipment, and if this wasn't an elaborate hoax, what else remained?

There had to be another explanation.

He considered there was something exceptional about Lindsey, besides the way she looked, smiled, and laughed. When he pictured her in his mind, it sent a rush of warmth cascading through his body.

Boy, I got it bad.

But what if Lindsey somehow saw the future? Many people claim such ability. Perhaps she was a modern-day Nostradamus.

Keith grabbed his phone, and several messages from Aric popped up. He swiped them off-screen, then opened the browser and typed a search for local fortune tellers. The results generated a long list of names. As he scrolled through them, Keith noticed most referred to their *'entertainment value and availability for corporate events.'* He omitted those listings from consideration. He wanted someone who at least made a pretense at legitimacy. When he reached the middle of the list, one result caught his eye and resonated.

"Find your connection with the future."

Her name was Madam Taliya, and he called her.

She answered on the first ring.

"This is Madam Taliya," she said. Her voice was deep and soothing.

"Hi, um, I was wondering if I could ask you a few questions," Keith said.

"A reading is thirty-five dollars," she said.

"Well, I'm not looking for a reading," Keith said. "I was hoping I could talk to you. It won't take long, I promise."

"I'm sorry," she said. "Appointments are available only to paying clients. Are you sure you don't want a reading? I sense an urgency in your voice, a longing. Am I right?"

Keith paused a moment before answering. "Well, yes," he said. "I guess."

"This involves a young woman, whom you have met under strange circumstances?"

Goosebumps broke out on his flesh as a chill passed through him. "Yes."

"I sense you have questions about her, which you fear asking."

"That's right."

"You should visit Madam Taliya. Meeting face to face, I can view your aura and read your tarot cards. You will feel better, I assure you."

"Okay," he said.

"Tomorrow morning, ten o'clock?" she said.

"Well, I have to work. Is there any chance we could meet now? I realize it's getting late, and I'm sorry. But I believe you can help me."

"And time is of the essence?"

"Yes."

There was a momentary silence as she considered his request.

"All right," she said. "You have my address?"

"Yes," Keith responded.

"Bring cash," she said. "Madam Taliya doesn't take cards."

He ended the call feeling perplexed. He had never dealt with a psychic before and thought the whole idea seemed preposterous. But in just a matter of seconds, she seemed to sense the precise details he'd experienced. It was uncanny.

A sense of certainty washed over him.

This must be the answer.

He toggled his phone back to the home screen, pressing the icon for Uber and requested a ride.

●

Keith arrived at Madam Taliya's apartment twenty minutes later, his mind whirling with questions. He realized he wasn't sure how he wanted this to go.

Overhead, heavy clouds had drifted in, obscuring the moon and diffusing its radiance. An icy breeze cut through his clothing and made him shiver. He zippered up his coat and walked to the building, climbing the steps and approaching the intercom panel. He searched for her name and finding it, pressed the button twice and waited. The voice he recognized from the phone, crackled through the speaker.

"Yes?" she asked.

"Um, hi. I'm Keith, I called you a little while ago," he said.

"Take the elevator to the fourth floor," she said through the intercom.

The speaker clicked, followed by the buzzing of the door. He pulled it open.

Keith entered the elevator from the lobby, stepping on carpeting stained and frayed. As he pressed the button for the fourth floor, the doors closed, revealing graffiti scratched into the metal.

As he reached his destination, he stepped out into a long, dimly lit hallway. Halfway down he saw a door open, and a middle-aged woman stepped out, wearing a flowing black dress revealing ample cleavage. She beckoned to him. As he approached her, he heard the muffled sounds of televisions and music playing behind the other doors.

Madam Taliya smiled at him. Her long hair was raven black, matching her clothing. Multicolored tattoos of flowers and strange symbols covered her arms.

As he entered her apartment, the aroma of burning incense enveloped him. Candles flickered, and Keith spotted a small round table in the living room with two wooden chairs opposite each other. A well-worn deck of tarot cards sat in the middle of the table casting a shadow.

"Hello, Keith," she said.

"Hello," he said, reaching out to shake her hand. She had long, thin fingers with a flawless manicure. Her skin was cool to the touch.

"May I take your coat?" she asked.

Keith set his backpack on the floor and unzipped his jacket. She took it from him and placed it on a hook at the back of the door.

"Did you bring my fee?" she asked.

Keith nodded, reaching into his pants pocket, removing the cash and handing it to her.

She checked the amount and then tucked the bills in her brassiere, smiling as Keith's eyes followed her hands. "Safer than a bank," she said and winked. "Shall we get started?"

Keith nodded.

She gestured to the table, and he moved over to it with her following behind.

As he sat, she came around the other side of the table taking one of the lit candles from a shelf against the wall and placing it in the center of the table. She sat down, and its flickering light cast her in a warm glow with alternating shadows. She reached her hands across the table, palms up.

After an instant, he realized he needed to do the same.

Her fingers had a firm grip, and Keith found it a challenge to look into her eyes.

"You are nervous," she said, it wasn't a question.

He nodded and focused on the deck of cards.

"Look at me, Keith," she said, and he complied.

"It seems like you see straight through me."

She held his gaze. "This is your first reading?"

"Yes," Keith said.

She was quiet for a moment, never breaking eye contact. He wanted to but resisted the urge.

"I see much in your aura, Keith. Anxiety, confusion and a great desire for answers, yes?"

"Yes," he whispered, locked onto her dark, penetrating eyes.

"You have protective spirits around you, guiding you. I also sense the energy of a young woman. She is dark and mysterious. You have questions about her?"

"Yes," Keith said.

"What do you want to know?"

"Is she like you?"

Madam Taliya blinked. "What does that mean?"

"Can she view the future?"

Her grip tightened on his hands, and she leaned in closer, her gaze intensified.

"Perhaps," she said. "Why do you ask this?"

"She talks from the past," he whispered.

Madam Taliya released her grip. Her brow furrowed and her eyes flared. "Is this girl deceased? Are you communicating with a spirit?"

"No. It's a recording," Keith said. "A videotape I found and watched. She could hear me and respond to the things I said. But the recording is old. I don't know where she is now. But I'm trying to understand how such a thing could be possible."

Madam Taliya sat back in her chair. "Spirits in this world connect to us," she said. "Space and time have no impact on them. These souls bond to us for reasons we cannot understand. I have never heard of the communication you described. But if you're asking if such a thing were possible, I would have to say yes. Your aura suggests you have experienced something profound. I don't know how it happened, but it is real. There are mysteries in this world that defy understanding. They are gifts bestowed on us, and we have the responsibility of accepting them, with gratitude, and not question their source or origin. Something special has happened to you, Keith. I believe it is your destiny."

Keith sat there, staring at the flickering candle attempting to process her words. Did she mean it, or was she only saying what he wanted to hear?

"Would you like a tarot card reading? It may provide additional guidance for you," she said. "It's only twenty dollars."

"No, thank you. I appreciate your help," Keith said. He stood and extended his hand to her, she took it, holding firm with both of her own.

"Whatever you experienced, it's a real thing. But you asked if this young woman is like me. She isn't. What I do works on feelings, emotions. I glimpse the path a person should follow. But I can't carry on conversations with people from the future. I don't know what allows something like that to happen, but it is something unique and special. Like, true love."

Keith smiled and nodded, attempting to take back his hand, but her grip tightened.

"Be careful," she said. "I sense you have suffered before. There's a great sadness around you, and I fear it may return." She released his hand. "I wish you luck in your quest. I see you traveling far, but paying a heavy toll. The universe forever strives to maintain balance. Love cannot exist without loneliness. To cherish joy, we must endure pain."

She leaned over and blew out the candle.

Chapter 12

Visalia, California
May 9, 1989, 3:59 AM

Lindsey's clock radio triggered at 4:00 AM filling her room with the sound of The Bangles singing "Eternal Flame." She slapped the top of the alarm, turning it off before it awoke anyone else in the house.

She sprang out of bed and checked the camcorder batteries she left charging overnight. Both showed a full charge. She tossed them into the bag with the camera, the tripod and a blank tape, already labeled *Tape #5*, surrounded with a border of hearts and smiley faces.

Dressing in the darkness, she pulled on a pair of jeans and a David Bowie concert t-shirt, grabbed the duffle bag with her recording gear, and proceeded down the hall, cautious to not make any noise.

She exited the house through the back door in the kitchen, and closed it with care, wary of the sound of the latch, then hurried to her car, parked on the street. She tried the ignition three times before the engine fired to life. She popped the transmission into gear and drove off.

Traffic was nonexistent at that early hour, and she moved through the town and onto the highway without delay. She always cherished the time before dawn. As a young girl living in Hawaii, her father would often awaken her while darkness still lingered, and bring her out to the beach. He would set a blanket on the sand and hand her a breakfast sandwich he'd prepared himself, along with a cup of hot cocoa for her, and a coffee for him.

They would enjoy their breakfast, listening to the lapping waves. Their hair tousled in the warm breeze as they watched the horizon transition into the colors of a new day. The memories of those mornings were like a warm embrace for her. Lindsey missed her father more than she wanted to admit, but remembering their time together kept him close to her heart.

●

She arrived at the park at 5:45 AM and already saw the indigo blue breaking on the horizon. From the front seat, she grabbed the camera bag, locked the car, and ventured into the forest. Her destination was a clearing at the top of a small hill, surrounded by Sequoias with the dawning eastern skyline as her backdrop.

As she unpacked the camera, she snapped on a battery, powered the unit up, and loaded in a fresh tape. Once secured to the tripod, she aimed the lens at the horizon, now a gorgeous shade of crimson. In the foreground, the giant trees framed the shot. She pressed record and panned around at a slow rate, providing a full view of her surroundings. When she finished, she stepped out from behind the camera and sat on a rock a few feet in front of it. She opened her arms wide and smiled.

"Welcome to my secret spot," she said. "Are the colors in the sky visible?"

For an instant, she felt a tinge of nervousness as she waited for a response. Then, in her mind, she heard a soft gasp and Keith's voice. "Wow," he whispered. "It's magnificent."

"I wasn't sure if the camera captured it," she said. "The viewfinder is black and white."

"Where are you?"

"The park I mentioned," Lindsey said.

"Are those Sequoias?" Keith asked.

"Yes," she said, and jumped up, moving behind the camera again, tilting the tripod upward, and showing the tremendous height of the trees. "I wanted to share this place with you."

"The trees seem to go on forever," he said in hushed amazement. "That's the most beautiful thing I've ever seen. I wish I were there with you."

A smile spread across her face. "You are," she said, and Keith laughed. She returned the camera to a level position, fixed on the horizon, and scurried back to her rock. "Am I in the frame?"

"Yes," Keith said. "But I must correct my earlier statement. *You* are the most beautiful thing I've ever seen."

Lindsey flushed. "You are a charmer, aren't you?"

"Not usually," he said. "I'm shy and uncomfortable around most people. But something about you, Lindsey, or I should say, *everything* about you makes me feel like a different person."

Behind her, the sun crested the horizon in a radiating blend of yellow and pink.

"I wish I didn't need all this equipment to talk to you," she said. "Sometimes I worry you're only a part of my imagination."

"I'm real," Keith said.

"I hope that's true," Lindsey said. "But ever since I was a little girl, I escaped into my imagination whenever things were scary, like when my parents fought. With paper and crayons, I'd hide in the closet for hours, making up stories, inventing people and places. Guess I've always used make-believe to help me cope. It makes me wonder if that's what I've done with you."

"This is more than imagination, Lindsey. I'm not creative enough to invent something like this, even though I've tried. There was a children's book my mom used to read to me when I was maybe four or five years old. She would sit down on the carpet in the living room, cross her legs, and I would crawl into her lap, lying back on her belly. She wrapped her arms around me and kissed the top of my head while holding this book. *The Adventures of Oba and Nim* by Edith Kinsley. Do you know it?"

Lindsey shook her head. "No, but I love the title."

"It's the story of these two characters, Oba and Nim. Oba is a Hope, and Nim is a Dream, and they traveled through this incredible world of imagination, on a walking flower named Lola Daisy." Keith laughed. "It's remarkable I still remember. I haven't thought about that book in a long time," he said.

"It sounds lovely."

"And you want to hear something amazing?"

"Of course."

"Edith Kinsley, the author of the book, saved my life."

"Seriously?"

He chuckled. "Yup. In Manhattan for my tenth birthday. We were on our way to the biggest comic shop in the city where my parents had promised me *anything* I wanted. I was oblivious of crossing signs and ran into an intersection."

Lindsey gasped.

"It had snowed that morning and coated the streets. This huge delivery truck jammed its brakes when it saw me, but it skidded on the snow and couldn't stop. I just froze."

"What happened?"

"This lady grabbed the hood of my winter jacket and yanked me out of the way. It turned out to be the author of my favorite book. What are the odds? My mom kept hugging and thanking her."

"That's incredible."

"And you know what's funny? I've never told anyone that story before."

Lindsey laughed. "Why not?"

"It's embarrassing. I nearly got flattened by a truck."

"So why did you tell me?"

"I don't know. It just felt natural."

Lindsey smiled and shifted her sitting position. "I bet your mom loved that book too."

"My most cherished memory of my mom is her reading those stories out loud. They made it seem like anything was possible. There were saber-toothed penguins, a pink dragon that pooped-out diamonds, talking flowers, pure imagination. It made me want to make up my own stories. But when I tried, nothing came out. It was so frustrating."

"It's possible," Lindsey said. "You need to learn how."

"No," Keith said. "There isn't a creative bone in my body."

"Creativity and imagination are different things. You need to set your mind free. I close my eyes, block out the surrounding chaos, and repeat this phrase: *Sail to serenity.* Soon my mind would whisk me away to someplace wonderful."

"You make it sound easy," Keith said.

"It is. What's easier than thinking of something?"

"When the world closes in on me, I can't focus on anything else. The worry and fear become overwhelming."

"That's called the logic brain," Lindsey said. "My senior year of high school, we had this artist provide a presentation on creativity. Her name was Julia Cameron. And she talked about how our brain has two parts, the logic part, and the creative part. She said the logic brain is where self-doubt lives. To free the potential of the creative side of your mind, you need to lock up the logic side, and let your creativity run wild, without judgment. It's why authors aren't supposed to write and edit at the same time."

Keith laughed. "*Write drunk, edit sober.*"

Lindsey smiled. "Exactly! Master that, and you can imagine *anything.*"

"That sounds incredible. But I'm not wired that way. I can't do that," Keith said.

"That's logic brain talking. You need to block it out while your imagination flows. Otherwise, it will tell you how stupid daydreaming is when there are worries everywhere. Life is about balance. Pressures and responsibilities will always be there. It's important to make time for play."

"That's my connection to video games and comics. They're my escape."

"But that's immersing in other people's art. You need to create things yourself too," she said.

"I've tried. I once had an idea for a cool superhero, but as soon as I started working on it, I realized it sucked."

Lindsey cocked her head to the side and gave him a stern look. "Logic brain," she said. "There's no question you possess the ability for creativity. You need to find your niche."

"You have it all together," Keith said.

Lindsey burst out laughing. "I am so far from having it together. My logic brain is gnawing away at me right now because I can't figure out how to use my creativity to earn a living. My mother is pushing me into a career in accounting." Lindsey shuddered. "Ugh, accounting. It's like a trap, baited with something tempting — a job and stability — which sounds good. But I'm certain if I take it, the trap will snap shut, and that's where I will stay until I die. There are all these magnificent things bouncing around in my head, but they'll never see the light if I follow this path."

"Does she understand you want to pursue your dreams?"

"She knows, and she doesn't care. It's as if she's figured out a way to chain her creative mind to a wall, and now she's forgotten about it. She is 100% logic brain, and to her, I'm foolish for considering anything *other* than accounting. She wants to turn me into a Vulcan, and I want to run away, screaming."

Keith chuckled. "Did you just make a *Star Trek* reference? You are perfect," he sighed.

She covered her face and laughed. "Aren't Vulcans all about logic?"

"Yes, they are."

"It reminds me of a tune. Do you know the band, Supertramp?"

"Yeah," Keith said.

"I love 'The Logical Song.' The singer shares how he saw the entire world as beautiful and simple when he was young. But as he grew up, everyone insisted he stop living in a fantasy and face reality. That was my experience living in Hawaii when my parents fought all the time. I didn't want to deal with how things were changing. Music helped me with that."

"What other music do you like?" Keith asked.

"I love Queen, David Bowie, Tina Turner, U2, Kate Bush, Peter Gabriel," she shrugged. "There are tons. I make mixtapes and play them on my Walkman all the time. Music is another form of escape for me," she blushed. "You can see I do *a lot* of escaping - music, books, daydreaming... talking to you."

"Am I part of your escape?" Keith asked.

"Oh, yes," she said, with a smile. "You're a good listener. Girls like that."

The rising sun, a half-circle of incandescent orange light on the horizon, cast long shadows into the forest.

"How much tape do we have left," Lindsey wondered aloud, and stood to cross to the camera, her silhouette blocked the sun, and the surrounding glow was angelic. She stepped in front of the lens, craning her neck, checking the viewfinder. "Almost out." She stepped back into view and waved. "Until next time."

Then the tape rewound.

Chapter 13

Keith sat watching the random static flickering on the television monitor, feeling bittersweet. When Lindsey said she wished she could speak to him all the time, it made him warm and fuzzy. But by watching *Tape #5* (after telling himself he would wait), he knew only one recording remained, and feared he might not find any more. Keith was adrift in these thoughts when a knock on his apartment door startled him back to reality.

"Open the door, man. The food's getting cold," said Aric from the hallway. "Keith, you in there?"

He snatched a dirty t-shirt from the pile on the floor, and covered the videotapes from Lindsey, then stepped to the door and opened it.

"You okay," Aric asked. "You look a little pale, I mean more so than usual."

"I'm fine," Keith said.

"Well, let me in dude, I brought you a late night snack." He held up brown bags, stained dark with grease. "Burritos and chimichangas, baby." Aric pushed passed Keith and entered the apartment. "I couldn't tell if you were home. Your bike's missing, but the lights were on." He set the bags on the coffee table and peeled off his coat. He spotted the monitor, flashing static on the screen, and looked back at Keith. "Did I interrupt a porn session? If so, you might want to wash your hands first."

"I wasn't watching porn," Keith said.

"Nothing to be ashamed of, man. Perfectly natural."

"I wasn't," Keith repeated.

"Well, why are you all worked up? I sent you texts about getting together tonight, and you didn't even respond. It's like you..." Aric stopped and looked again at his friend. "Met someone," he finished, and then lowered his voice to a harsh whisper. "Is someone here? Is that why you're acting spooked?"

"Yes, no. I don't know," Keith said and shook his head.

"What's going on, man?"

"Something weird."

"Tell me."

Keith only managed a shrug.

"C'mon, the suspense is killing me."

"When I was at the flea market on Saturday, I found a videotape from a camcorder. And when I played it, something surreal happened."

"What?"

"I had a conversation with a girl thirty years in the past."

Aric just stared at him.

"Seriously, it happened," Keith said.

"But that makes no sense."

"I agree. But it still happened. We spoke to each other, she could hear me. She's an incredible artist and-"

"When did she make this tape?" Aric interrupted.

"1989," Keith said.

"Dude, she would be a grandmother now," Aric scoffed.

"I'm aware of that," Keith said.

"Show me the tape. I want to see this."

Keith froze, unsure what to say. He wondered what might happen if he played the tapes for Aric. Would the magic disappear?

"I don't think it's a good idea," Keith said.

"Why not?" Aric asked.

"Because I'm still trying to understand what's happening."

"You mean how you're using VHS tapes to Skype with a girl from the 80's?"

Keith shrugged. "I figured you wouldn't understand."

"Are you messing with me? You can't be serious. Do you know how crazy this sounds? I was worried you might find a girlfriend, but I didn't expect you'd be *Driving Miss Daisy*."

"I have to ask you to leave," Keith said and saw the hurt spread on Aric's face.

"What? Come on, man. What's really going on?"

"It was a mistake telling you. Please go."

"I brought you chimichangas, man. If your videotape girlfriend got you food, it would have decomposed by now." Aric snatched the bags off the coffee table and stormed out.

●

Keith couldn't sleep that night. His mind raced with thoughts and concerns which refused to settle down. He felt guilty for turning his friend away, confusion regarding the videotapes, and fear about losing Lindsey. He pictured her and felt a palpable, consuming desire to run his fingers through her long, flowing hair, pull her close to him, and kiss her soft and deep. A warm, beautiful thought cratered by the realization she made her recordings before Keith was born. She could be anywhere, now. Married, with kids, or maybe, like Aric said, a grandmother. Keith groaned. The whole thing was crazy, yet he couldn't give it up.

Then he remembered the questions from the video technician.

What would happen if he played the tapes again? Might there be a different conversation with her?

He jumped out of bed and hurried to the equipment rack stubbing his foot on the corner of the couch. He dropped to the floor, clutching his toes in agony. After a moment of wincing, he pulled himself up and powered on the equipment. As he searched through the small pile of Lindsey's tapes, he found the first one he watched, and loaded it into the VCR, hitting the rewind button. When it finished, he reached to press play but hesitated.

What if he was only meant to view the tapes once? Could watching it a second time somehow ruin the magic and sever their connection? Or might it provide him with an entirely new conversation with her? How could he know?

He took a deep breath and pressed the play button.

Static on the monitor switched to the view of Lindsey's bedroom. She came out from behind the camera wearing the same baggy INXS t-shirt and sweatpants she wore when he first saw her.

"Lindsey? Lindsey, can you hear me?" Keith asked, observing her, hoping for a new reaction.

She didn't respond, sitting on the bed, as she did before.

"Lindsey, I'm worried I won't be able to find your other tapes," Keith said, leaning close to the monitor, the light from the cathode ray tube bathed his face in a blue glow.

"Here we are, tape number three, and I'm no closer to my goal than when I started," she said, just as before.

"Please, Lindsey. Say something different. Tell me you can hear me," he begged.

Instead of responding, Lindsey lowered her voice, sounding like a television announcer, and said, "Previously, on Lindsey talks to herself," then returned to her normal tone, and giggled. "Insecurity, uncertainty, and a nagging mother. Did I forget anything?"

Everything was the same. The recording didn't change.

Keith turned down the volume but kept watching her, captivated by her beauty. He wanted these tapes to provide him an endless connection with Lindsey, but that wasn't how it worked. These were real chats. They happened once and then became a memory.

Then he remembered only one more tape remained unwatched, and a crippling sadness gripped him as he realized it might be their final conversation.

His arms hung at his side as he stumbled back to his room and dropped onto the bed with a long, low sigh, knowing full well rest would elude him.

●

Keith was awake, lying on his back, staring at the ceiling through bloodshot eyes, when his alarm clock triggered at 6:00 AM. Drained and exhausted, he climbed out of bed and went to shower. The steaming hot water did little to clear his head.

At the sink, wrapped in a towel, he wiped the foggy mirror and tried to shave. But his bleary eyes refused to focus, and he nicked his neck in several spots. He grabbed a tissue, tearing off small pieces, and applied them to the cuts, when he heard his cell phone ringing in the bedroom.

He hurried to the nightstand, picked up the phone and checked the screen. Caller ID showed the number of Duncan Distributors.

"Yes? Hello?" he said, holding the phone to his ear as drops of water from his wet hair dripped onto his hand.

"I'm trying to reach Keith Nolan," a male voice said.

"Speaking," Keith said.

"This is Rory from Duncan Distributors. I got a message saying you wanted to buy videotapes?"

"Well, I'm looking for specific camcorder tapes, the small ones. You shipped a few to vendors in Hoboken, New Jersey. Do you have others? They're very distinctive. Each one has a label with illustrations on it. They're unique and sure to stand out."

"Look, pal, we have *thousands* of tapes in our warehouse. But they aren't sorted by title or type. They're piled in massive bins. I couldn't tell you what's in there even if I wanted to, which I don't. If you want to go sifting through them, knock yourself out, but I suggest you pack a lunch. Maybe supper too."

"Really?" Keith said.

"Why not?"

"Thanks. I'll be there later today."

"Whatever," he said, and hung up.

Keith dried off the phone and navigated to a travel app called AVIATO. He booked a seat on a flight to Ohio, leaving at 10:00 AM, then tossed the phone on the bed and packed a bag.

At 6:45 he called work. He expected to reach the receptionist and give her the message he wouldn't be coming in. The phone rang three times, before being answered, by Mr. Witlicki.

"Blair," he said.

Keith felt an instant wave of nausea sweep over him.

"Mr. Witlicki," he said sounding weak. "This is Keith Nolan. I can't come in today. I'm sick with the flu."

"Are you joking? I told you yesterday we need all hands on deck. It's the *busy time!*"

"I'm very sorry, sir, but I'm throwing up, and dizzy. If I tried to work in this condition, the whole office might get sick."

"Get a doctor's note, Mr. Nolan, because, without one, you'll be looking for a new job. Do you understand?"

"Yes, sir, Mr. Witlicki."

"Good," he said and slammed the receiver, terminating the call.

Keith placed his phone in his pocket and covered his face with his hands, massaging his temples.

●

His duffel bag packed with a change of clothes, toiletries, his laptop, cell phone, headphones, a notebook and pens, Keith pulled on a coat and exited the apartment.

As he headed for the stairwell, the door to the next apartment opened. The tenant, an elderly woman, named Louise Fusco, stepped into the hall. She was thin and frail, with a full head of white hair, and skin like parchment.

"Keith?" she called out to him.

He turned to face her. "Hi Mrs. Fusco," he said.

"I'm so sorry to bother you, but could you help me with something?" She noticed the duffel bag. "But if you're in a hurry, that's okay. It's not a big deal. I don't want to be a nuisance."

"I'm heading to the airport to catch a flight, but I have a few minutes, what is it?"

She led him into her apartment, and Keith stifled a cough from the overwhelming aroma of Jean Nate and Marlboro cigarettes. An ashtray filled with crushed, lipstick-stained cigarette butts, sat on the arm of the couch.

"My daughter is stopping over today," she said. "She wanted to pick up photos of her father. I have them stored in a box on the top shelf of the closet. But I'm not strong enough to get them down. Would you mind?"

"No problem," he said.

Keith found the box, overstuffed and pushed to the back of her bedroom closet shelf. With some effort, he reached and pulled it down, careful not to spill any of the photos. He carried the box into the living room and set it on the coffee table in front of her couch.

"Thank you so much, Keith," she said, beaming with appreciation. "You're a good boy." She picked up her wallet and pulled out a ten-dollar bill, handing it to him.

"No," he said, shaking his head.

"Take it," she insisted, waving the bill in front of him. "Buy yourself a cup of coffee."

Keith relented, taking the money and smiling. "Thank you, Mrs. Fusco."

She patted him on the shoulder. "Where are you off to?"

"Ohio," he said.

"Have a safe trip."

"Enjoy your visit with your daughter," he said.

She shrugged. "I'll try," she said.

●

With his flight delayed for two hours, Keith had ample time to wander around the airport shops. There was a Brooks Brothers store, stocked with clothes he would never wear, costing more than he would ever spend. A Travelmart offered trinkets and souvenirs, along with travel-sized options of toiletries to help people avoid looking homeless while traveling.

A music and movies store sold over-priced CDs and DVDs. He spent twenty minutes browsing their selections, and found a few intriguing items, but refused to pay $26 for an album he could order online for $11.

Next, he visited the bookstore, a micro-version of a Barnes & Noble. Stacked at the entrance were new, hardcover releases from John Grisham, Michael Connelly, and Nora Roberts. Keith drifted over to the paperbacks section and scanned the covers, recognizing a few of the authors - Stephen King, James Patterson, and Michael Crichton - but most were unknown to him.

Keith realized he should read something other than comic books, but old habits die hard. He blamed his aversion to novels on high school teachers who forced him to read books like *Silas Marner*, which he found painfully dull.

He finished high school without ever experiencing the joy of books like *Huck Finn, To Kill A Mockingbird*, or *Catcher In The Rye*. Instead, he scanned copies of CliffsNotes® making a crib sheet he used to pass the tests. The ploy worked, he graduated English class but failed to develop a love, or even an interest, in literature.

He continued browsing the paperbacks until something caught his eye. It was a copy of *The Joy Luck Club* by Amy Tan, the book Lindsey mentioned in her first tape. Without hesitation, he pulled it off the shelf and brought it up the register.

Keith took the book from the clerk's hand, refusing a bag. As he exited the store, he opened to the first page and read. The experience of exploring a story he knew Lindsey loved, connected him to her, and for the first time in his life, he savored reading a book.

He was halfway through it when his flight prepared for final approach.

●

By the time Keith landed in Ohio, the autumn sun was creeping toward the western horizon. He rented a car, a sky-blue Ford Focus that reeked of cheap aftershave, and set out for the distribution center.

It was an enormous warehouse in an industrial park forty minutes south of Columbus. The front office was a tiny, claustrophobic room with a half-wall, decorated with a placard proclaiming DUNCAN DISTRIBUTORS - *We can get it for you!* Behind the wall, a young woman with short, dark hair, sat beside a phone, typing at a computer terminal.

"Can I help you," the woman asked when Keith entered.

"Yes," he said. "Rory said I could look through the inventory of videotapes because it involves a missing person."

"Oh, um, can you hold on a moment?"

She walked to a door at the back of the room, opened it and spent several moments speaking to whoever was inside. She nodded and then returned to Keith, with a stern look on her face.

"Are you a police officer?" the receptionist asked.

"No," Keith said.

"I'm sorry, but I can't allow you inside unless you have a warrant."

"But Rory told me on the phone it would be okay for me to check for other copies of her tapes. That's why I traveled from New Jersey this morning to come here."

"I'm very sorry, sir, but we do not allow our inventory to be searched by the public. We are a distribution center. If you would like to purchase our inventory of videotapes, I can help you with that."

"How many tapes do you have?" he asked.

The woman turned to her computer terminal and typed a quick search.

"We have 7432 tapes in the warehouse."

"And the cost?"

"Our bulk discount price is just 50 cents a tape."

"So, I have to pay you $3500?"

"If you are interested in getting all the tapes."

"I don't want *all* the tapes. I'm just looking for camcorder recordings from a girl in California."

"I can't help you with that, sir. Do you want to purchase a smaller quantity? We can sell them in lots of one hundred."

"Can I sell back the tapes I don't need?"

"Of course," she said with a pleasant smile. "Our purchase rate for VHS tapes is five cents each."

Keith threw his arms up in frustration.

"Is there anything else I can help you with today?" she asked.

Keith leaned in close to her over the half-wall with a pleading look in his eyes. "What if I told you this was about love? Do you believe in love?"

The woman looked confused. "I thought you said it was a missing person case."

"It is. Well, sort of. This girl is missing from my life, and I need these recordings to find her. Can't you help? Please, I'm only asking for a little compassion."

The office door at the back of the room opened, and a smart-dressed woman in a red business suit strode toward the counter. She had a gaunt face and narrow eyes. "Is there a problem, sir?"

"No. I'm only hoping for a little human kindness."

"I beg your pardon?" the second woman snapped. "We have informed you of our policy on these matters. You may purchase, or you may leave. Otherwise, I'll call the police."

"He said it's about love," the receptionist said in a gentle tone.

"Love is a grave mental disease," replied the woman in the suit, without the hint of a smile. She kept her eyes fixed on Keith. "Are you buying the tapes or not?"

His stomach clenched as if kicked.

"I don't have $3500," he said just above a whisper.

"Then we're finished. Good day."

With his shoulders slumped, he turned and left the office.

When he reached the rental car in the parking lot, he doubled over, vomiting his airline breakfast and splashing it on his shoes. He stood up and then retched again.

With the entire contents of his stomach emptied onto the asphalt, he wiped at his mouth and climbed into the driver's seat.

What am I going to do? The question echoed in his head like a mantra.

He knew Lindsey's tapes shipped from this location. But it wasn't a guarantee any remained, and without spending a fortune in cash, he couldn't be certain.

For a moment he considered ways of breaking into the facility and avoiding the surveillance cameras. He expected there would be a security guard, and it was while calculating options for subduing and restraining the guard, that he questioned his sanity.

Defeated and devastated, he started the car and drove to the airport.

Chapter 14

Visalia, California
May 10, 1989, 7:13 PM

In her bedroom, with the door closed, Lindsey loaded a blank tape into the camera and pressed the record button. Dressed in a tight-fitting top and Capri pants, her hair resting on her shoulders, she sat close to the lens. Outside her window, the setting sun cast shadows against the glass.

"Hi, Keith. How are you?" she asked and smiled, awaiting his response.

But the only sound was the gentle whirring of the camera's recording mechanism, as the red light glowed.

"Hey, are you there?" she asked, sliding closer to the camera. "Can you hear me? Please be there." She bit her lower lip, uncertain what to do. "Keith? Where are you, Keith? Please answer," she begged.

Someone pounded on her door.

"Lindsey, let me in," her mother demanded from the hallway.

Rising, Lindsey stopped the recording and opened her bedroom door. Phyllis stood there, dressed for a night out, her makeup applied thick and her hair styled and sprayed into place. An invisible cloud of cloying perfume encircled her.

"Who is *Keith?*" Phyllis asked.

Lindsey remained silent.

"You called out to someone named Keith. *Who is he?*"

"He's no one, mom."

She pushed passed Lindsey and entered the room.

"Is it someone you are dating? How are you talking to him in here?"

Phyllis spotted the camera. She turned back to her daughter with a stunned look. "You aren't making sex tapes are you?"

"No!" Lindsey shouted.

Phyllis stepped close to the camera and pressed the eject button. The tape popped out, and she grabbed it.

"What are you doing?" Lindsey cried.

"I don't approve of you hiding in here, making illicit, secret recordings for this Keith ruffian."

"Give me back the tape, mom!"

"No," she said. "I'll check it later. I want to confirm no shenanigans are happening when you lock that door. In the meantime, I'm going to a Barry Manilow concert with the girls from work. I won't be back until late. There are leftovers in the fridge. Wit is working until 7:00 after that he'll be at the Polish Club playing cards with his brother. If you need him for any reason, the phone number is on the fridge."

Lindsey shook her head. "I won't."

"You might want to take this time alone to reflect on your future. Decisions need to be made soon, Lindsey. Think about the life you want and what needs to happen to attain it. Because this," she gestured to the camera. "This is no way to spend your time, sweetheart."

She leaned in and kissed Lindsey on the cheek, leaving a large smear of lipstick which Phyllis wiped away. Without another word she walked out of her daughter's room, taking the tape with her.

Lindsey dropped onto her bed, grabbing a pillow and clutched it, while her jumbled mind chased too many thoughts. Furious with her mother's actions, she wanted to escape, get out of the house and leave everything behind. But with no money and nowhere to go, they had her trapped. She ached to speak with Keith, and couldn't understand why he hadn't responded to her on the tape. Was he hurt, or worse? Fear gripped her with the possibility the magic between them had run dry, and he couldn't return to her again. What if he decided he no longer wanted to waste time on a girl from the past and met someone else? Emptiness unlocked in her, and she groaned.

But her eyes opened wide when an alternate explanation popped into her head. Maybe the reason Keith didn't respond was that Phyllis confiscated the tape. What if her mother's actions prevented that recording from reaching the future?

Lindsey relaxed, deciding to test her theory in the morning. She'd buy more tapes and try again, away from the prying of her mother.

The clutter and commotion of her thoughts quieted, and she slipped into a restful sleep.

●

It was 1:14 AM when Lindsey was woken by the sound of the front door closing. As she opened her eyes, she realized the lights in her room were still on and hopped out of bed to switch them off. She was in no mood to talk to her mother again that night, especially after Phyllis probably spent the evening receiving endless suggestions from her coworkers about how to deal with her "troubled" daughter.

Lindsey climbed back into bed, pulling the covers over her, as footsteps echoed in the hall. She held her breath, not wanting to make a sound until they passed. But instead of continuing up the stairs to the master bedroom, they stopped at her door.

Ah, shit. Keep walking, please.

The knob to her bedroom door turned, and the latch popped, allowing a low creak to escape from the hinges. Lindsey clenched her eyes tight and tried not to move at all. The door opened further, and light from the hallway spilled into her room.

What's wrong with her? Why does she want to argue with me in the middle of the night? Can't she leave me alone?

The footsteps entered her room and continued to the side of her bed.

She remained frozen. Sure any movement on her part would invite Phyllis to launch another verbal attack. Lindsey prepared for the overpowering scent of her mother's perfume.

A hand stroked her hair, and with it came the vile odor of vodka and sweat.

It was Wit.

Lindsey's heart hammered in her chest.

The mattress bowed as he sat on the bed beside her, still stroking her hair. She wanted to scream, to leap up, flailing her arms and howling like a banshee. Instead, abject fear held her frozen.

The weight on the mattress shifted, and with horror she realized he was lying down beside her, on top of the comforter, making a low, unintelligible mumbling.

Seized by panic, she clenched her eyes shut even tighter, as tears squeezed out the corners of her lids.

His hand moved from her hair to her face, and his dirty fingers stroked her cheek. She fought back the bile rising in her throat. Her mind raced, trying to think of something — anything — that was within reach she could use as a weapon against him. But the nightstand had only her clock radio and the comic books.

She wanted to hear Keith's voice encouraging her to stay brave and strong, to assure her everything would be all right.

Wit's fingers slipped down to her neck, and she knew she was running out of time. She had to do something but remained paralyzed with fear.

The touching stopped.

She held her breath, cheeks slick with tears, terrified for what was next.

Then she heard snoring. Wit had passed out.

Lindsey rolled out of bed, landing on the floor. She retreated to the corner of the room and recoiled in disgust. The light from the hallway illuminated his shape, still dressed in his soiled work clothes. She cringed watching him roll into the spot on the bed she'd occupied and continue to snore.

She crept out of the room and hurried through the hall to the living room closet. Lindsey dug through the top shelf, cluttered with hats, scarves, and gloves, to find what she was looking for: her mother's Polaroid camera.

When she came back, she stopped at her open bedroom door, lifted the camera, peered through the viewfinder and pressed the red shutter button. The electronic flash illuminated the room in a stark, burst of bright light. The motor of the camera ejected the photo from the slot in the front.

Despite the noise and blinding light, Wit's body failed even to twitch.

Lindsey turned her attention to the photograph.

For several moments there was no discernible image, only a block of gray. But within moments the picture developed, revealing her bed, with Wit lying in it, his mouth hanging open and a stream of a drool leaking down his face.

Lindsey took the photo into her mother's empty master bedroom and stuck the photograph into the edge of Phyllis' makeup mirror.

When she returned to her room, Lindsey grabbed a change of clothes and shoes, and brought them into the bathroom and dressed. She grabbed her keys and slammed the front door behind her.

As she got behind the wheel, her emotions escaped, and she sobbed, resting her head on the steering wheel, allowing herself to purge the fear and horror. When it ended, she wiped at her eyes and nose, started the car and drove off into the darkness.

Chapter 15

The flight from Ohio seemed liked a blurred movie running at half speed. Keith felt hollow inside like something had ripped a massive piece of him out, and only the gaping hole remained.

He arrived at Newark Liberty International Airport at 8:35 PM, wandered outside and climbed into a cab.

"Where to, pal," the driver asked, observing Keith from the rear-view mirror.

"221, 14th Street, Hoboken," Keith said, staring out the foggy window, and kept silent the rest of the 45-minute ride home.

He stepped into his apartment, dropped his bag on the floor and closed the door. As he stepped into the living room, he saw the remaining unwatched tape from Lindsey sitting on top of the VCR. He stood there for several minutes, just looking at it.

What am I going to tell her? How do I admit I failed?

The depression consuming him was too intense. He knew he couldn't talk to Lindsey in his current condition. If this were to be their last conversation, he needed a clearer head.

He walked into the bedroom and fell onto the mattress.

Hours later, she came to him in a dream.

Sunlight gleamed through her hair, bathing her in a golden glow. Her eyes sparkled as she smiled and laughed.

They were on a pristine beach. She wore a bikini, dancing through the turquoise waves breaking onto the white, glistening sand. The water tickled her toes, and she laughed again, then noticed Keith wasn't smiling. She rushed to him and knelt at his side.

"What's wrong?" she asked, wrinkling her brow and biting her lower lip.

"I failed," he said. "And now I'll never see you again."

She moved in and embraced him. The heat coming off of her skin was intoxicating. He breathed deep, savoring the aroma of the sea in her damp hair.

"We have something special," she whispered in his ear, and he felt her warm breath on his neck. "Nothing can keep us apart. Not even time."

She pulled back, taking his face in her hands and stared deep into his eyes.

"You feel that too, don't you?"

He couldn't summon words and managed only a nod.

She moved her hand to his chest, over his heart.

"I will be *here*, forever."

The dream shattered with the blaring of his alarm clock.

He crawled out of bed, showered, shaved, dressed and had a quick breakfast, all while remaining in an emotional fog. Muscle memory sent him out of the apartment and down to the bike stand before he remembered he no longer had a bike.

He hailed a cab and arrived at work twenty minutes early. At his desk, he sorted through the day's responsibilities and organizing the scattered clutter of folders and documents on his desk.

Mr. Witlicki's office door opened, and he stepped out. "Nolan," he said, standing in the doorway. "Feeling better?"

"No, honestly, I'm not," Keith said. "But at least I'm here."

The boss nodded. "Where's your doctor's note?"

Seized with panic, Keith swallowed hard. The events of the previous day had pushed the memory of the note out of his head.

"I couldn't get out of bed. Sorry, but I didn't make it to the doctor."

"Is that so?" Witlicki asked. "You didn't hear me pounding on your door?"

Keith's stomach soured with the realization his boss went looking for him. "Um, I guess so," he said with a shrug.

"That's interesting," Witlicki said. "Because my pounding on your door was so excessive, it brought out your next-door neighbor to ask about all the commotion. She's a sweet lady. What's her name? Mrs. Fusco, I think it is. Anyway, *she* told me you weren't home."

Keith went white.

"Yeah," Witlicki continued. "She said you caught a flight to Ohio or something. But before you left, you helped her take down old photos of her husband. She thinks you are a 'nice' boy."

Keith put up his hands. "I can explain, Mr. Witlicki."

"You're fired, Nolan. Pack your things and get out."

"I'll make up the time."

Witlicki turned back into his office and closed the door behind him.

Chapter 16

Sequoia National Park
Three Rivers, California
May 11, 1989, 5:30 AM

A knock on the driver's side door of Lindsey's car startled her awake. She recoiled in fear, clutching herself as the events of the previous night crawled back into her memory. Confused for an instant, she wasn't sure where she was or how she got there.

Then she saw the park ranger holding a flashlight, tapping on her door.

"Young lady," he said. "Are you all right?"

She struggled to clear the cobwebs from her mind and nodded. "Yes," she said through the closed window. "I'm fine."

"Sorry, but the park prohibits sleeping in vehicles. I have to ask you to leave."

She rubbed her eyes and asked, "What time is it?"

The ranger checked his watch. "5:30, miss."

"Okay," she said. "Is there a breakfast diner nearby?"

The ranger nodded. "Head west on Route 198 and take the first exit. Then follow the signs."

"Thank you," she started the car and drove out of the parking lot.

When she left her mother's house, her instinct was to run away, just keep driving until the gas tank went dry. But she had almost no money, and no one to take her in. The thought of returning to her mother's house made her skin crawl. What else could she do?

With a new day dawning in the sky overhead, nothing seemed any better, and no choices had come clear.

She followed the highway to the first exit and saw signs for a diner. When she pulled into the parking lot, the place was already bustling. She parked and picked up her sketch pad and a pencil, then proceeded inside.

The diner looked like a massive silver bullet lined with windows. Red neon lights trimmed the edges. Bright fluorescent bulbs illuminated the interior, decorated in white Formica and red vinyl booths. The heavy scent of fried food permeated the air.

There was an open seat at the counter, and Lindsey sat down, placing her pad in her lap. A waitress came over, wrapped in a white apron stained with spots of grease, holding a steaming pot of coffee. She had blond hair pulled up and tied with a red handkerchief. Her name tag identified her as Polly.

"Rough night, sugar?" she asked.

Lindsey managed a nod.

"Coffee?" Polly hoisted the pot and gave it a slight shake.

"Do you have tea?" Lindsey asked.

"Sure." Replacing the coffee on its warming tray, Polly grabbed a pot of hot water and a tea bag. She returned to Lindsey, dropping the tea into a cup and splashing it with the hot water. "Did you wanna see a menu?"

"No, thank you," Lindsey said.

Just as Polly was turning to walk away, Lindsey stopped her.

"Do you have a pay phone?" she asked.

The waitress pointed toward the end of the counter, near the cash register.

"Thanks," Lindsey said. She sat for a moment, lost in her thoughts, as she stirred her cup with a spoon. She checked the clock on the wall over the grill and saw the time was 6:05 AM.

Too early to call, she thought.

She signaled to Polly again, who hurried over smiling.

"I need to stay here for a little while, but I can't afford to order anything else. Is that okay?" Lindsey said in a lowered voice.

The waitress stepped closer to her. "No problem, sweetheart. Do you need anything?" she asked, with concern in her eyes.

"No, thanks,"

Lindsey opened her drawing pad and flipped to a clean page. She sketched her cup of tea and the spoon resting on the edge. The noises of the diner, clinking dishes and utensils, the sizzle from the grill, and the din of multiple conversations, became a protective force field around her, muffling the barrage of thoughts threatening to push forward in her mind. She focused only on her drawing.

The illustration of the teacup started as a realistic still-life. But soon she added fantastical, tiny, furry creatures with over-sized ears and eyes, using the mug as a pool, and the spoon as a diving board. When she finished, Lindsey flipped to another page and sketched the grill, with its spatters of grease, an egg cooked sunny-side up with its edges bubbling, and an apron crumpled on the counter. To this image, she again added her fictional creatures, this time with them using the egg's yolk as a trampoline.

When she next checked the time, it stunned her to see it was 8 AM. The restaurant was still bustling, but the crowd filling the booths and lining the counter was an entirely different group of people from when she came in.

Lindsey walked to the phone, fished a dime out of her purse and dropped it in the slot where it landed with a clank. A dial tone buzzed out of the receiver. She pressed zero, the tone vanished, followed by an audible click.

"Operator," said a female voice on the other end.

"Hello," Lindsey said. "I need to place a collect call, please."

"The number?"

Lindsey told her.

"And your name?"

"Lindsey," she said.

"One moment."

The number dialed, then another click, and the connection completed. It rang several times without an answer, and Lindsey realized it was still too early to call. She was about to apologize to the operator, telling her she would try again later when someone picked up.

"Hello," said a woman's voice, scratchy from sleep.

"I have a collect call from Lindsey, will you accept the charges?"

"From who?" the woman asked.

"Lindsey," repeated the operator.

"Is my father, there?" Lindsey interrupted.

There was a sigh from the woman, followed by the receiver dropping onto the nightstand. Lindsey heard a muffled conversation and then the sound of another voice.

"Hello," her father said, with a tone of concern.

"I have a collect call from Lindsey, will you accept the charges," the operator said again.

"Yes, yes," he said.

"Thank you," the operator said before disconnecting herself from the call.

"Lindsey?"

She took a second before responding, not wanting him to recognize the shaking in her voice. "Hi, dad," she got out.

"Are you okay? What's wrong?"

"Nothing," she lied. "I wanted to hear your voice," she said. That part was true.

"It's 6 AM here, blossom. We were sleeping. Are you sure you are okay?"

"Sorry, dad, I only wanted to say hi. Guess I didn't notice the time. I'll let you go. Apologize to Gwen, for me."

"Hang on, Linds. What's going on with you? Have you started college?"

"I'm trying to figure out what I want to do."

"That's okay. Sometimes it takes a while."

"Yeah."

"How's your mother doing?"

Lindsey shrugged, uncertain of how to answer. "The same," she said.

"But you're *sure* you are okay?" he asked.

"Yeah, Dad. But I was wondering, do you think it might be possible to come and visit you for a little while?"

There was a hesitation in his response. "I wish I could say yes, honey, but you know the situation. I'm sorry. I still need to work some things out. Maybe by Christmas, huh?"

"Sure. Love you."

"I love you, too, blossom," and then he hung up.

Chapter 17

Hoboken, New Jersey
October 25, 2019, 11:09 PM

Keith stumbled along the sidewalk, overlooking the Hudson River. The glass spires of Manhattan twinkled in the moonlight, as he took another long swig from the bottle of rum he carried, wrapped in a brown bag. The burning at the back of his throat as he swallowed made him wince. Through his blurred vision, the city skyline appeared like an almost magical land.

With half the bottle empty, his head buzzing and his feet heavy, he stumbled to a park bench and collapsed onto it.

"How can I be so stupid?" he slurred.

"I ask that all the time," said a voice that gave Keith a jolt.

He turned to see a vagrant fishing through the trash can beside the bench. Dressed in a heavy wool coat, tattered and matted with dirt. A shaggy beard of gray and brown obscured his face. The cap that covered his head had tufts of matted hair poking out from beneath. His eyes moved to the bottle Keith was holding, and he smiled, revealing his missing front teeth.

"Whattya got there?" he asked coming around to the front of the bench.

Keith shrugged and offered him the bottle. "Want some?"

The man nodded. "Drinking alone is sad."

As he sat down on the bench, Keith handed him the bottle and watched as he took a long pull from it.

The man swallowed and grimaced. "Rum?" he asked. "What are ya, a pirate?" He cackled with laughter. "Supposed to mix this with sody pop. If ya wanna drink somethin' straight, vodka's a good choice. Or scotch. Or tequila."

Keith shrugged. "I didn't know what to buy. I don't drink much."

"But yer drinkin' tonight."

Keith nodded. "Yes, I am." He took the bottle back and swallowed another mouthful. He extended his hand, "I'm Keith."

"Jack," the man said, shaking Keith's hand. He took back the bottle. "So what brings you out here to drink from a bag? Girl trouble?"

"No. Yeah. Beats me," Keith said shrugging. "Sort of. I met a girl. She's beautiful and smart, and funny. And beautiful."

"She's got you repeatin' yourself," Jack said with a wink. "That's usually a good sign."

"Yeah. I'm crazy about her," Keith said and shrugged. "But she's not here."

"She's far away, huh?"

Keith chuckled. "Yeah, you could say that. 3000 miles and thirty years."

"Distance ain't no obstacle for love. Do ya love her?"

Keith attempted a nod. "I can't get her out of my head. She's in my dreams, but I barely know her."

"That's easy. Learn more about her."

"I tried," Keith said. "It cost me my job."

"Oh," Jack said. "You got lots of reasons for drinkin'."

"How can you tell if someone is right for you, Jack?"

Jack shrugged. "Dunno," he said. "Never met someone who was."

"She makes butterflies in my belly. I'm lightheaded when I look at her," Keith said.

"Are ya sure it's not the rum?" Jack asked and chuckled.

"No, it happens when I'm sober."

"Sounds like you got it bad, kid."

"I've thought the *exact* same thing."

"If I was you, I'd tell her all this stuff."

"She's in the past."

Jack shrugged. "Never too late," he said. "If yer still breathin' you can tell her how ya feel."

"I'm not good with rejection."

"Who is?" Jack asked.

"My first love was a girl in high school. Her name was Skyler. She had blond hair, blue eyes. A pretty girl."

"Go on," Jack said with a nudge and took another swig.

"We dated our junior and senior years. I expected we would be together forever."

"You poor bastard."

"For two years I worked odd jobs after school. Cut grass in the summer, shoveled snow in the winter and saved every penny I earned. A few days before graduation, I took it all to the jewelry store. $480 bucks. And I bought an engagement ring."

Jack handed the bottle to Keith, and he took a swallow.

"After graduation, at a party at her friend's house, I gave her the ring," Keith said.

"And?" Jack asked.

"She laughed because she thought it was a joke. Told me it was sweet I felt that way, but we were too young, and she wanted to go to college first. So, I told her I would wait for her and keep the ring safe. She went to school in Boston. I came here to Jersey. I would call her, write letters, and send cards. But soon I stopped hearing from her. A year later her friend told me Skyler had met someone else and was too afraid to tell me."

"Afraid?" Jack said.

"Yeah, she said I was *too* sensitive and that I might kill myself, and she didn't want that guilt on her conscience."

"So, instead, she stomped your heart flat and chucked it into a meat grinder."

"Yup."

"Bitch," Jack said. "Did you get drunk that night too?"

"Oh, yeah. I woke up in front of some stranger's house, vomiting into a sewer grate. Pretty much haven't drunk since, until tonight."

"Was it rum, that night too?"

"No, Jack Daniels, courtesy of my roommate. That's why I tried something different tonight."

"Well, there's no doubt you're better off without that woman. I'm sure it didn't seem it then, but rejectin' your offer was the best thing she could ever do for ya."

"Right," Keith said. "Thanks, Skyler!" he hoisted the bottle high, before drinking from it again. He closed his eyes as he swallowed, then sighed. "What am I going to do, Jack?"

"Dunno," Jack said. "But I can tell ya from experience, the answers not in that bottle."

"No?" Keith asked.

"Nope," Jack said. "You should let me hang onto it for ya, and you go home and sleep it off."

Chapter 18

Three Rivers, California
May 11, 1989, 9:13 AM

Lindsey sat behind the wheel of her Maxima, leaned back against the seat with her eyes closed, facing a crucial decision: go home or run away. Her emotions were like a bucking bronco, violent and volatile, threatening to throw her off at any instant.

Her conflicted mind had two warring factions, on one side her lingering juvenile feelings, and on the other, her emerging sense of adult responsibility.

She knew the grownup choice was confronting her mother about what happened and demanding Phyllis do something about it. But as soon as Lindsey prepared what she wanted to say, the memories of Wit's hands on her came rushing out of her subconscious and threatened to send her shrieking.

The childish side of her wanted to avoid it all, saying to hell with her mother, and Wit. It told her to drive as far as she could until the gas ran out, then ditch the car and walk, or maybe hitch a ride.

She slapped down that thought. It didn't require much imagination to guess what awaited a teenage runaway with no money or transportation. With dreaded confidence, she understood it would make her experience with Wit only a warm-up to the horrors she would encounter.

As much as she hated it, the only choice for her was to go home. But the memory of Phyllis slapping her crept into her mind, and Lindsey felt her hands tightening into fists.

Stay in control, she thought to herself. *You can do this*.

She battled back her growing anger by thinking about Keith.

Taking a deep breath, she exhaled, opened her eyes and started the car.

On her way back to the highway, she spotted a Radio Shack and pulled into the parking lot. As she entered the store, she saw a long row of televisions all set to MTV, displaying Paula Abdul's choreographed moves as she sang "Straight Up." The store was empty except for a salesman behind the counter, playing a handheld video game.

Lindsey made her way past a display of camcorders and spotted what she wanted, blank videotapes. She pulled a 2-pack off the wall and checked the price: $8.99. The salesman came around the display and flashed a smile. He wore a leisure suit and an overwhelming amount of Aqua Velva. As he noticed Lindsey's disheveled appearance, his smile receded.

"Can I help you with something, Miss?"

She held up the package of tapes. "Do you have any that are less expensive?"

"We do, however, I wouldn't recommend them. If you buy cheap videotapes, your home movies won't last as long. Those tapes you're holding are manufactured with the highest quality components and are guaranteed to last twenty years. Cheaper tapes will degrade much sooner. Aren't your memories worth a few extra dollars?"

Lindsey imagined Keith watching her tapes and realized this wasn't a time to act stingy.

She nodded and followed the salesman to the checkout counter.

●

The drive back to Visalia was swift with only light traffic as most morning commuters had already reached their destinations. Lindsey pulled off the highway at her exit and traveled the remaining distance to the house in a few minutes.

When she pulled into the driveway, the first thing she noticed was the front yard littered with Wit's belongings. She exited the car, surveying the debris. His clothes, electric razor, and fishing magazines covered the grass.

The front door burst open, and Phyllis tossed out an armful of other items, before spotting Lindsey. Her face shifted from fury to relief and back to anger.

"Where have you been? I've got the police looking for you! Jesus Christ, why didn't you call me?"

They stood there for several moments only staring at each other in silence. Finally, Phyllis walked back into the house.

Holding the desire to flee in check, Lindsey walked up the front steps, avoiding the piles of clutter. Reaching the front door, she could hear Phyllis on the phone.

"Yes," her mother said. "She came back. She's safe. I wanted to let you know you can stop looking for her."

There was a pause before she continued. "She seems okay, but I will ask her. Thank you," and she hung up.

Lindsey stepped into the living room. The house looked like a raging storm had swept through it, with overturned chairs and shattered glass glinting on the floor.

Phyllis stepped closer to Lindsey. Her hair mussed and streaks of mascara marring her cheeks, she wiped at her nose with the back of her hand as she looked at Lindsey.

"Are you..." she choked back her emotions and cleared her throat. "Are you okay?"

Lindsey nodded.

"Did he..." and then Phyllis allowed the tears to run.

"He tried," Lindsey said. "But he passed out before he could."

Phyllis opened her arms and embraced her daughter. "I'm so sorry," she sobbed.

Lindsey allowed her mother to hold her but didn't hug her back.

"Where is he now?" she asked.

Phyllis backed away, wiping at her face with both hands. "At his brother's. They're coming later to get his things out of the yard. The rest of his shit is going in the trash."

"You are divorcing him, right?" Lindsey asked.

Phyllis nodded, sniffling.

"Did he hit you?" Lindsey could see a bruise forming on her mother's left cheek.

"I did that myself, tossing his things out."

"It looks like there was a struggle in here," Lindsey said glancing around the room.

"I said he didn't hit me," Phyllis said, dismissing it. "The police want to know if you want to press charges against him."

Lindsey thought about it for a moment and shook her head. "I want him out of our lives."

Phyllis nodded. "It won't be easy for us," she said.

"We'll figure it out." Lindsey stepped over the broken glass on the way to her room.

Chapter 19

Keith woke with a throbbing headache and a parched mouth. The drawn curtains held the bedroom in darkness, but trickles of light seeped in at the edges of the window. He staggered out of bed and into the bathroom. Running the faucet, he ducked his head into the sink and drank water in giant gulps, only stopping when he felt the sloshing in his stomach.

Still dizzy from the rum, he steadied himself in the doorjamb and returned to the bedroom. When he reached the end of the bed, he sat down, head in hands.

The ache of desperation pervaded his senses. He'd lost his job and with it, his income. He wouldn't be able to pay rent or buy food. His mind yanked him back to the dumpster he searched, and a chill slid through him. His grip on his life was slipping and would soon spiral out of control.

Before long I'll be homeless. I'm pathetic and useless. Thank God my parents didn't have to see me this way. He dropped to the floor, hanging his head.

But despite the threat of being destitute, the thought creeping to the forefront of his mind was his broken promise to Lindsey.

Failing to recover more copies of her tapes left him consumed with self-loathing. He hated himself for not keeping his pledge and the penalty was an unrelenting gnawing guilt.

With his eyes closed, he rubbed his aching head and stretched his neck. When he opened his eyes, he saw the stack of long boxes holding his comic collection, and a realization struck him like a thunderbolt.

If he sold the books, he could use the money to find the rest of Lindsey's recordings. It would have been an unfathomable idea just a week earlier. Those books were a cherished connection to his childhood and his parents. But meeting Lindsey had altered his entire life and changed him. From the moment he first saw her move into position in front of the camera, a chemical reaction triggered inside him. She permeated his waking thoughts and penetrated his dreams. He would do *anything* to keep her in it.

Before she entered his world, he'd been oblivious to the void in his soul. She was the missing piece. With her, he was whole.

Confident in his new plan, he smiled for the first time in days.

He popped up from the floor and rushed into the living room. Lindsey's final videotape rested on the equipment rack. He picked it up and loaded it into the adapter, then slid it into the VCR and pressed the play button.

Snow and static flashed on the monitor then flickered with the image of Lindsey's room. But things were different. Her unmade bed, with the sheets and comforter crumpled in a ball on the mattress, were only the first sign.

When Lindsey stepped in front of the camera, Keith gasped with shock. She was different too, mussed hair and dark circles under her eyes. She looked exhausted, devastated. Keith moved close to the monitor, placing his hands on the flickering glass.

"Lindsey," he whispered. "Are you okay?"

She nodded and then wiped at her swollen eyes. "Better now," she said and tried a laugh.

"What's wrong," he whispered.

She sniffled and avoided looking at the camera.

"Had a bad night," she said.

"Do you want to talk about it?"

She shrugged, fighting back the tears. "I thought I did. I called my dad, woke up his girlfriend. But when he got on the phone, I heard the worry and concern in his voice, just like I hear now from you," she shrugged again. "I couldn't do it. I couldn't tell him, and I can't tell you."

"Please don't block me out," Keith said. "Did someone hurt you, Lindsey?"

"He tried, but nothing happened. It was terrifying, and I was so alone and helpless. *I fucking hated that!*" Lindsey shouted.

"I wish I could have been there for you," he said, as his voice cracked. "Tell me how to find you. I want to be by your side, Lindsey, to protect you."

She released a bitter laugh. "And how old will I be when you do?"

"Who cares about that? I *need* to be with you. Don't you feel that too? Be honest."

She closed her eyes and shrugged again.

"Are you even alive in 1989?"

Keith remained silent.

"I've realized I need to take responsibility for my life," she said. "I dragged my feet on deciding my future because I feared it would be the wrong one. But that indecision put me in the situation I found myself in last night. If I had taken control of my life, had a place of my own, it wouldn't have happened.

It's time for me to grow up. I can't keep talking to you like this. It's silly. You're not even real. You're just in my head."

"This is not a fantasy," Keith said. "I don't know what is happening, but I crawled through a dumpster to find these tapes. I traced them back to a distributor in Ohio. It cost me my job, but I don't care. Now I have a way to find the rest of your tapes, and I'm leaving in the morning to get them. You're all that matters. We're meant to be together, Lindsey, I sense it in my soul. *You are the one for me.*"

Tears flowed down Lindsey's cheeks, dampening her lashes with each blink.

"You're in my head and my heart, Keith. It's like you're perfect. And that's logical if I imagined this whole thing. But in the real world, no one is perfect."

"I'm *not* perfect. I'm a grade-A fuckup. But don't give up on us. I can't imagine my life without you."

"You need to work on your imagination, Keith."

"If we could agree on a safe place for you to stash the tapes, then I could find them and we -"

"There aren't any other tapes, Keith. This will be the last one. It's time I grow up, stop hiding and face the world. But I'll be forever grateful to you. You made me believe I'm special."

"You *are* special, Lindsey," he whispered, tears sliding down his face. "Don't do this, please."

She tried to speak, but the words caught in her throat, she wiped the tears from her cheeks.

"I will find you, Lindsey. I swear it. Please tell me how to find you. Where are you in California?"

"Visalia," she said. "241 East Sunnyview Avenue. But I don't think we'll be here much longer."

"I will be in California tomorrow."

"Yeah, tomorrow for you, but how many years is it for me?"

Before Keith could answer, Lindsey turned off the camera.

Chapter 20

Keith stood by his bedroom window, watching and waiting for his cab to arrive. A concrete sky, overcast with dense clouds shaded everything in gray. The trees lining the street had all shed their leaves. Only their bare, bony branches remained.

His duffel bag rested on the crumpled sheets of the bed, packed with clothes for a three-day trip. Stashed at the bottom of the bag beneath the three shirts and four pairs of underwear, was the black velvet jewelry box from his desk.

Stacked beside him was the pile of boxes containing his comic collection. Keith's hand rested on the top lid, and his fingers unconsciously caressed the cardboard. In his mind, the memories of each book's acquisition played out. Birthday gifts, Christmas mornings, countless weekends spent scouring flea markets, yard sales, and antique shops.

He felt a presence in the room with him and tried to imagine his parents. He wondered, *what would they think of this?* He struggled to remember them with clarity, but the images he conjured were blurry and faded. Time had robbed him of the details of their faces, so instead, he clung to the feelings.

With perfect recall, he remembered being loved and protected. The way his dad would hug him after getting home from work, hoisting Keith into the air and then pulling him close. With his face pressed against his dad's shirt, breathing in the fragrance of his aftershave and lingering pipe smoke. Or the aroma of his mom's cooking coming from the kitchen and filling the house with a magical blend of olive oil, onions, and garlic. Keith remembered how after dinner, he'd help clear the table, while his mother washed the dishes. When it was finished, she held him close to read him stories, and the faint scent of garlic still clung to her. To him, it was like perfume.

Outside, the cab pulled up to the curb and honked its horn twice.

It took Keith four trips up and down the stairs, to bring the collection out of the apartment and into the back of the waiting taxi. He stacked each box with care and closed the trunk.

"Whatchya got there?" asked the driver.

"My childhood," Keith said and then gave him directions.

They arrived outside the comic shop ten minutes later, and Keith instructed the driver to wait for him. He climbed out of the cab as the trunk popped open and grabbed the first box. As he carried it across the sidewalk, the frosty autumn air turned his breath into foggy vapor.

The shop was tiny, dark and packed tight with shelves and tables brimming with comic books. A life-sized cardboard cutout of a snarling Wolverine, his claws extended, greeted Keith as he entered. He set the box down beside the register.

"What's this," asked the kid behind the counter. He was skinny and tall, with bad skin and a thick shock of red hair.

"My X-Men collection. I need to sell it," Keith said.

The clerk removed the cover from the box and flipped through the books.

"Holy shit," he said. "Are you serious?"

"Yeah," Keith said, and walked out to get the next box.

By the time he had brought them all in, the clerk held an electronic tablet, checking prices of the books.

"You have a lot of key issues here," said the clerk.

"I have *all* the key issues. It's a complete run."

"That's insane," said the kid. "Why are you selling them?"

"It's time," Keith said.

The clerk replaced the box's lid and looked at Keith. "Man, I got to be honest with you. I can't afford to buy these from you. You know how much this run is worth, right?"

"Yeah," Keith said. "I do."

"I could take them in on consignment."

Keith shook his head. "I need to get cash up front for them. I'm taking a trip, and I'm a little light right now."

"All I have on hand is $1800 in the safe."

"I'll take it," Keith said. "You have the books as collateral. And we can work out an arrangement for selling them."

"Let me draw up the paperwork, and we'll get you on your way," the clerk said.

Chapter 21

The campus of the Visalia community college, known as COS, College of the Sequoias, was only a ten-minute drive from Lindsey's house. The buildings all featured rounded corners in clean, white stucco and expansive windows painted with teal trim. A pillared walkway wrapped around the facility with neatly tended gardens filled with succulents and ornamental rocks.

As she entered the admissions building, Lindsey found the office teeming with people, both young and old, milling about, chatting and filling out forms.

The scene was claustrophobic and chaotic. Lindsey resisted the urge to dash outside, retreat to her car and drive off to the park. After several minutes a plump woman in a rose-patterned dress, with a wide smile, greeted Lindsey.

"Hello, young lady," she said. "How can I help you?"

"I need to enroll in the fall semester," Lindsey said, as her imagination pictured an enormous metal trap, set and baited with a degree in accounting.

"Wonderful," said the woman, pulling out pamphlets and documents from beneath the counter. "Do you know what classes you are interested in?"

"The accounting program," Lindsey said in a flat tone.

"It's a popular study," the woman said, handing the papers to Lindsey. "Here is the course description, along with the recommended classes and schedule. You must fill out the registration and paperwork about financial aid."

Lindsey found an open spot among the throngs and filled out the registration form. She remembered something she'd been told once, about friends made in college being the closest friends in a person's life. She wondered if that were true, and if so, were any of these people, huddled together, going to be her friends later in life? There were girls with big hair, moussed and sprayed into sculpted manes, boys dressed in flamboyant clothes, with bright colors and matching sneakers. There were adults too and a few seniors, but no one stood out as someone who would even talk to her, let alone become a lifelong friend.

When she completed her paperwork and handed it in, the clerk informed her the school would be in touch over the next few weeks and classes started September 5th.

Instead of exiting to the parking lot, Lindsey walked the hallways of the main buildings. Her time in high school had been a lonely, miserable experience, and she doubted community college would be any different.

Perhaps some people are doomed to be alone.

She considered it might explain Keith's origin. Lindsey needed something positive in her life while facing the uncertainty of her future. Keith, she thought, was her coping mechanism, a way to escape the pressures she felt every day and providing her a modicum of happiness.

For her, to think she was conversing with someone from the future was nuts. But was Keith a figment of her imagination? She *heard* him, his breathing, his laughter, and his sighs. But that wasn't possible, she reasoned.

A tiny voice in her head asked, *what if it is?*

This internal debate was tearing her up. The rational part of her mind decided she needed to knock-off the charade and stop behaving like a child. It was time to be an adult, no more talking to imaginary boyfriends, and get on with her life.

As she drove home from the college, the question remained about what to do with her videotapes. Should she throw them away? That would be the most dramatic way to show her newfound will and strength. Toss them out and don't look back. That's how an adult would handle it, she thought. Make a symbolic gesture to herself about embracing the reality of her life and not clinging to some silly fantasy.

When she arrived home, she entered her room and pulled the shoe box containing her recordings, out from under her bed. Her fingers left tiny imprints in the fine layer of dust collected on the cover. She picked up the box, tucked it under her arm and made her way outside, to the trash cans lined beside the garage. With her free hand, she opened a can and prepared to toss the box inside. But before she could, an involuntary muscle movement made her lift the lid, and she glanced at the videotapes inside. Her skin flushed with warmth as she sensed Keith again. Not his words, it was quiet except for the soft, lonely call of a mourning dove perched in a sycamore above the garage. But Lindsey sensed Keith's presence, as an almost imperceptible tingle of electricity.

He's real, she thought and at that moment understood she couldn't dispose of the tapes. If she did, it meant Keith, wherever he might be, would never find them, or her.

She tried to wrap her head around the idea, and somehow it made twisted sense. Of all her recordings, only once did Keith not respond to her. That happened with the tape Phyllis confiscated and threw away. Lindsey couldn't hear Keith because her mother's interference separated that recording from all the rest.

If there was any hope of Lindsey and Keith getting together, even if it was far in her future, she had to figure out how to ensure Keith discovers the tapes.

Then she remembered something he said about a place in Ohio, and she dashed to her car.

●

Video Galaxy XIII, the local video rental store was next to a liquor store on Route 63. When Lindsey had been younger, Phyllis would bring her there to pick out movies to watch on a Friday night, or Saturday afternoon, but those visits seemed far in the past.

The building showed signs of aging, flaked paint, cracked windows and worn carpet. Shelves filled the store, overstuffed with movie boxes, organized by genre. Posters covered the walls, and several televisions hung suspended by the ceiling, playing an endless loop of movie trailers. A few people browsed the "New Releases" section, featuring multiple copies of *Three Men and a Baby*, and *Crocodile Dundee II*.

Lindsey approached the clerk, seated behind the counter, searching through the job listings of the newspaper.

"It's kind of quiet in here," Lindsey said.

"Yeah," the clerk replied. He was about twenty-years-old and still battling acne. "Blockbuster Video stole most of our customers. What can I do for you?"

"I have a weird question. Do you know the name of a place in Ohio that sells used videotapes?"

"We get our stuff new, from vendors in Los Angeles. We don't buy used tapes. But we have been getting junk mail from a place in Ohio offering to buy up old videotape inventories. Seems like a bad business plan, if you ask me."

"Do you remember the name of the place offering to buy tapes?"

"We got another flyer from them today, but I tossed it out." He turned to the trash bin and pulled out the pile of junk mail and flipped through them. "Here ya go," he said, and set down on the counter a maroon sheet of paper, proclaiming WE BUY USED VIDEO TAPES! SELL YOURS TODAY! As she scanned the rest of the advertisement, she found the company's name and address.

"Can I keep this?" Lindsey asked.

"Sure."

She folded the paper and slipped it into her purse. "Thanks," she said.

Her next stop was the post office.

Lindsey bundled up the shoe box with her recordings, stuffing crumbled newspaper inside to prevent the tapes from rattling. She wrapped it in brown shipping paper, taping up the ends, and addressed it to Duncan Distributors in Williamsport, Ohio.

After she paid the postage, she watched as the postal employee tossed the box into a shipping bin marked OUT OF TOWN.

That's it, she thought. *It's out of my hands now. If it's meant to be, it will.*

Chapter 22

Keith arrived at the airport and waited at the check-in counter. Due to the late hour, the concourse was quiet, and only a few people were ahead of him in line. When he reached the clerk, she checked his ticket and smiled.

"California, huh?" she said. "Hightailing to warmer weather before winter takes hold? You picked the right time to go."

"I'm sorry?" Keith said, not understanding her.

She pointed out the window to the barren trees in the courtyard outside. "All the leaves are brown," she said, humming the melody of *California Dreamin'*. "I'd like to get the hell out of here and escape to someplace beautiful."

She finished the check-in and handed Keith his boarding pass. "Enjoy your flight," she said.

Keith picked up his bag, tried to smile and walked to the TSA screening line. He passed through with no delay, entered the departure area and headed to his gate, strolling passed a lounge with people gathered around a television, watching hockey.

His mind reeled with a myriad of worries. What awaited him in California? Might she have forgotten him after so much time? Was it a fool's errand?

Outside the massive windows, was the airfield with jets being tended to by their crews, refueling and shuttling luggage.

As Keith reached the gate, his phone buzzed in his pocket. He removed it and glanced at the display. It showed a picture of Aric's smiling, bearded face. For a moment he considered ignoring the call and switching off the phone. Instead, he answered it.

"Hello."

"What the hell is going on, man? I was at the comic shop tonight, and they have your entire X-Men collection listed for sale. Why are you doing that?"

Overhead, a public address announcement blared from a speaker.

"Are you at the airport? Keith, what are doing, man?"

Keith sighed. "You don't understand."

"You're goddamn right," Aric said. "So explain it."

"I have to find her, Aric."

"The girl on the videotape?"

"Yes."

"The videotape from *thirty years* ago?"

"Yes," Keith said, trying to hold his anger in check.

"So, you sold the most valuable thing in your life, to find a girl who is now a geriatric bingo player?"

"I knew you wouldn't understand," Keith said.

"Because it doesn't make sense, man. You are throwing everything away. Is it true you lost your job, too? I stopped there to talk to you, and they said you'd been fired."

"It doesn't matter."

"Doesn't matter?" Aric asked, incredulous.

"Yes," Keith said. "Nothing else matters but her. You don't get it because you didn't experience it. I can't explain it to you. It's like faith."

There was silence on the other end. Then Aric took a deep breath and exhaled. "I know you think I'm just a big pain in the ass, Keith. But I am your friend, and I'm worried you're making a huge mistake. I'm trying to do everything I can to prevent it."

"I understand," Keith said. "And I appreciate it. I do. You're right, you are my friend, and I'm grateful for that. But as my friend, you should want me to be happy. Right? Well, for that to happen, I have to find Lindsey. She's the one. I've never been more certain of anything in my life."

Aric didn't respond. He knew there was nothing left to say.

Keith listened to the silence for a moment before speaking. "Are you still there?"

"Yeah," Aric said. "Send me an update, if you can."

"I will," Keith said and switched off the phone.

●

An hour later he boarded his flight, an enormous 767 jet, with two aisles separating three seating sections. Rows of double seats ran along each side of the plane, and a row of triple seats in the middle. Keith, carrying his bag and boarding pass, searched for his window seat. He found it, but a large, middle-aged gentleman in a parka occupied the aisle seat.

Keith stood there a moment, expecting the man to notice him and rise. Instead, the man sat rigid, with his winter coat zippered up to his neck and the hood pulled over his head. Keith cleared his throat to get the man's attention, but he refused to acknowledge Keith and continued to stare at the seat in front of him. With people gathered behind Keith, waiting for him to get out of the aisle, a few grumbled.

"Excuse me," Keith said, leaning into the man's field of vision. "I need to reach my seat. Do you mind standing up?"

The man made eye contact with Keith but didn't utter a word. He grimaced as he stood, and Keith pushed passed him and sat without thanking him, as the rest of the passengers moved to their seats.

With his seat belt fastened, Keith set his bag on his lap and gazed out the window to the tarmac, where the crew loaded the last of the luggage. Overhead, in the clear night sky, a brilliant crescent moon beamed.

Keith unzipped his bag and removed a pocket-sized, moleskin notebook tucked inside. A black ribbon sewn into the spine acted as a bookmark, and he flipped open to the pages it separated. There, in his messy handwriting, was the address Lindsey had given him. *241 East Sunnyview Avenue.*

He tried to imagine talking with her face-to-face, a conversation without gazing into a flickering television screen. What might she look like now? How will she react? He struggled to imagine it, but his mind was blank.

Then he recalled Lindsey's story about how she entered her imagination. He shifted in his seat, closed his eyes, ignoring the surrounding sounds, and whispered the mantra, *Sail to serenity.*

As he did, he visualized her better in his mind, made out the details of her skin, the tiny birthmark on her neck, just below the jawline. He saw the way her long, dark hair, cascaded over her shoulders, and the sparkle in her eyes when she smiled.

Can you hear me, Lindsey?

But she didn't respond.

Doubt seeped, telling him how foolish this was.

Please, Lindsey, say something.

A shove on his right shoulder shattered the image. He opened his eyes to find the man in the parka staring at him with a look of annoyance.

"Quit talking in your sleep," he grumbled. "It's very distracting."

For the rest of the flight, Keith sat in silence. After a while he returned the notebook to the bag and removed his headphones, plugging them into his phone. He opened his music app and selected a playlist called *Lindsey,* filled with her favorite artists. He pressed shuffle and Supertramp played "The Logical Song."

There is nothing logical about what I am doing. This probably doesn't end well for me.

But there was no stopping it now. The inexorable pull carrying him 3000 miles across the country, to chase a girl, now a woman, was inescapable.

I will find you, Lindsey.

●

By the time they started the final approach to LAX, Keith was bleary and drained, watching the dawning new day through red-rimmed eyes.

As the wheels of the giant jet touched down on California soil, a gentle voice at the back of his mind whispered, *I'm getting close, Lindsey.* He hoped the revelation might release a rush of euphoria, but the nagging doubt eating away at him prevented it.

He rented a subcompact car, requesting one with a navigational system, but none were available. Instead, he balanced his phone on the dashboard, using it as his GPS device. He entered his destination with no need to refer to his notebook:

241 East Sunnyview Avenue, Visalia, California.

After a quick calculation of the route, the app showed Keith had a three and a half hour trip ahead of him, based on current traffic conditions. *Welcome to Los Angeles,* he thought.

He considered stopping for breakfast at one of the countless fast food establishments he passed. It seemed he hadn't had a meal for days, but stopping was unacceptable. Nauseous from nerves, eating was impossible. And with Lindsey so close, he wouldn't waste any more time.

Settled in for the long ride, he switched on the phone's music app and set it to shuffle. Queen's "Somebody to Love" played, and as the lyrics started, Keith struggled to hold his emotions in check.

When he listened to Lindsey's music, it provided Keith another direct connection to her. But hearing the words and music, and riding the exact emotional roller-coaster of longing and loneliness she had, became overwhelming. He realized she had experienced these emotions for *three decades*. That was a prison sentence.

An all-consuming sadness engulfed him, and tears streamed down his face. He opened the window to let fresh air wash over him.

There's no way she waited for me, he thought with certainty. *How could she? Why would she?*

He pressed hard on the accelerator, and the engine revved, driving the speedometer to 85.

I don't know what I will encounter, he thought. *But whatever it is, I want to find out as soon as I can.*

The next song to play was U2's "With or Without You."
He fought hard not to ponder the lyrics as he sang along.

●

He arrived in Visalia at 9:15 AM, making better time than the GPS predicted because he exceeded the speed limit for most of the trip. As he pulled into the neighborhood, Keith saw the sidewalks bustling with morning activity, mothers pushing strollers, people walking dogs, everyone aglow in the California sunshine.

When he made the final turn onto Sunnyview Avenue, Keith's pulse quickened, and he felt dizzy. He pulled to the side of the road to regain his composure.

This is it, he thought, and the realization terrified him.

He leaned his head back, closed his eyes, and drew deep breaths into his lungs. When he felt his pulse rate returning to normal, he put the car back in drive, and rolled forward, looking for her residence.

And he found it.

It was a small Cape Cod style house with yellow siding and white shutters around the windows. A one-car garage sat at the end of the narrow driveway, with a blue Buick parked in front of it. The front door of the house was open reflecting sunlight into the living room through the screen door.

Keith parked across the street and switched off the car. As he reached for the door handle, he noticed his hand shaking, and clenched a fist to steady it. He mustered his will, popped open the door, and stepped out of the vehicle. As he did, a UPS delivery truck driving past almost hit him. The rush of air pushed him back against his rental car, ruffling his clothes and hair. His heart hammered in his chest.

He crossed the street, scanning the yard for anyone outside, but no one was around. As he walked up the driveway, he felt a weakness in his legs threating to bring him down in a heap. Sweat formed on his brow, and he wiped it away with the back of his hand. When he reached the sidewalk, he climbed the three cement steps and stood before the front door. The living room was visible, decorated with photographs in ornate frames, and a substantial collection of Hummel figurines displayed in an ebony hutch.

Keith took a breath and knocked on the door.

From inside a small dog yelped followed by the voice of someone trying to calm it.

"Just a minute," someone called from inside.

Keith's palms were slick with sweat.

A middle-aged man came to the door, dressed in a light green sweater and khaki pants. He had a handsome face and dark hair trimmed short.

He opened the screen door and smiled at Keith. "Sorry about that, had to put my Pug in the bathroom. She's tiny but vicious. She can lick you to death."

Keith should have laughed at the comment, it was the proper thing to do, but he froze, trying to process who this man might be. *Is this her husband*?

"Are you okay?" the man asked, a look of concern spreading on his face.

Keith shook loose from his paralysis. "Yes, I'm sorry," he said. "I'm looking for Lindsey."

The man's brow furrowed. "No one here by that name," he said. "You must have the wrong address."

"Is this 241 East Sunnyview Avenue?"

"It is," the man said with a nod. "But there's no Lindsey here, sorry."

"This used to be her house. How long have you lived here?"

The man thought for a moment, then called into the house, "Babe, what year did we move here?" He looked back at Keith and smiled. "I'm awful with dates."

From behind him, another man approached the door, placing a hand on the first man's shoulder. He was gray-haired and distinguished, with a well-groomed silver beard and piercing blue eyes. He looked through the door at Keith before answering.

"Who's asking?" he said.

"This young man is looking for someone named Lindsey, is that who we bought the house from?"

"No," he said. "Her name was Phyllis. We bought it in January 1990. I believe she had a daughter, but I don't know her name."

"Do you remember Phyllis' last name?" Keith asked.

"That was a long time ago."

"Is there any way to find out? Could it be on your mortgage paperwork?"

"What is this concerning?" the gray-haired man asked. "Why are you looking for her?"

Keith reached into the pocket of his coat and pulled out the black jeweler's case. "I have something that belongs to her," he said, opening the case and showing them the ring inside.

Both men gazed at the ring, sparkling in the morning light.

"Hang on," said the older man, before walking away.

"Do you want to come in?" asked the man in the sweater, stepping back from the door and gesturing to Keith to enter.

He hesitated and then stepped into the foyer. As he did, Keith's entire body tingled as if he sensed Lindsey's energy still lingering. *She was here*, he thought.

From the hallway, the dog continued barking.

"Princess, stop it!"

The older man returned from the hallway, holding a stack of documents. "Phyllis Udell. That was her name."

"Do you know where she might be now?" Keith asked.

The man shrugged. "No idea. She might be anywhere, maybe even passed on by now."

"Thank you," Keith said. "I appreciate your help. I'm sorry to have bothered you."

"Hope you find her," said the younger man. "That's a beautiful ring."

Back in the car, Keith snatched his phone from the dashboard and opened the Facebook app. At the search bar, he typed *Lindsey Udell* and hit return. Over a dozen matches popped up, and Keith screened them. Most were young girls, and he eliminated them as possibilities. But several had no image posted, or their biographical information was available only to accepted friends. He sent friend requests to all of them.

Then he typed a search for Phyllis Udell. The results yielded only one match, an older woman, with short-cropped blond hair, employed at the Visalia Senior Center. Keith found the address and set it as his destination.

Chapter 23

Six months had passed since Lindsey mailed off her recordings and returned the video camera to its carrying case. Her mother sold the house, moving them into a two-bedroom apartment on the other side of town. They spoke at length about where to go, with Lindsey suggesting Hoboken, New Jersey. But Phyllis wanted to stay.

"I have friends here," her mother said. "I don't want to run away again."

It didn't matter to Lindsey. She knew *her* time in the town would end soon. Once she finished her associate's degree, she'd be moving on. She hadn't decided where, but returning to Hawaii held an allure.

The college experience proved less stressful than she expected. Being in classes with adults instead of petulant teenagers made a huge difference. When people have to pay to learn, they seldom waste time on petty bullshit.

Keith still popped into her mind, and when he did, it was a welcomed surprise, like a visit from an old friend. There were no new conversations, she only remembered their time together and wondered where he might be, and if they'd ever meet face-to-face. Lindsey didn't obsess over it. The further away she got from the whole experience, the easier it became to dismiss it as a vivid trick of her mind, and there were now other things fighting for her attention.

The most exciting development for her was the change in her art. She explored a more whimsical approach in her sketches, creating silly, imaginary beings, most with wide, curious eyes, and sly smiles. A definite departure from the realistic form she'd developed and pursued as a teen.

After her classes concluded each day, she'd drive out to the roadside diner near the National Park, order tea, and finish her assignments. With whatever time remained, she put on her headphones, turned on her Walkman, and drew in her sketchbook until supper time when she returned home to the apartment.

While working on one of her illustrations, lost in the creative process, she felt a tap on her shoulder. Split Enz played "One Step Ahead" in her earphones, and she pulled them off and turned around.

"Excuse me," said a woman in her thirties, dressed in a gray skirt and matching blazer. She had a broad, warm smile and offered her hand to Lindsey. "I'm Gail Prescott."

"Hi, I'm Lindsey Hale."

"I'm sorry for being forward, but you are talented. I adore the style. May I see some of your other illustrations?"

Lindsey felt her face flush with embarrassment. "Sure." She handed the sketchbook to Gail, who flipped through it, pausing on several of the drawings and nodding approval.

"I'm a literary agent, and one of my clients is working on a manuscript that requires illustrations. We've been searching through portfolios, but nothing has clicked for us. These are impressive."

Lindsey stifled a laugh. "You must be joking," she said.

"Far from it. Have you ever sold any of your work?"

Lindsey shook her head.

"Do you have a portfolio?"

"No."

"Well, get one together, and quick." Gail pulled a business card out of her jacket and handed it to Lindsey. "Then call me as soon as you do."

"I don't even know what to include," Lindsey said.

"Do you have more examples of work in this style?" she asked, handing the sketchbook back to Lindsey.

"Yes."

"Gather up the best of it and call me. I'll help you organize it. How old are you?"

"Twenty."

Gail smiled again. "You have a bright future ahead of you, young lady." She patted her on the arm. "Call me soon, okay?"

Lindsey only managed a quick nod as the world around her spun in a blur. She waited until Gail left the diner and then squealed with glee.

Chapter 24

Visalia, California
October 27, 2019, 9:42 AM

The Visalia Senior Citizen Center, on the corner of North Locust Street and West Oak Avenue, was only a five-minute ride from Sunnyview Avenue. A vast, beige building with a green awning over the front doors and benches lined against the outside walls, it bustled with activity as folks entered or congregated outside chatting.

Keith parked his car and weaved through the crowd near the door. Inside, a chipper, blue-haired lady wearing a name tag identifying her as "NANCY" greeted him. She smiled at Keith as he crossed to her desk. "Ain't you a little young for this place," she said and chuckled at her joke. "What can I help you with?"

"I'm looking for Phyllis Udell," Keith said.

"She teaches a class on Wednesdays, so I don't know if she is around today," Nancy said. "Hold on a moment, dear." She stepped around the desk, craning her neck to look into a long hallway leading down the left side of the building. Halfway down the hall, a thin, gray-haired woman pushed a carpet sweeper. "Martha?" Nancy bellowed and then looked back to Keith. "She doesn't hear well," she said, before shouting for her again. This time the woman turned to look at them.

"Did you call me, Nancy?" Martha asked in a soft voice.

"Yes, dear. Is Phyllis here today?"

"Who?" Martha asked, cupping a hand to her ear.

"*Phyllis!*" Nancy shouted.

Martha nodded and pointed at them. "Rec hall," she said.

Nancy waved. "Thank you!"

Martha returned to her sweeping.

"Good news, I guess she is here. Follow me." Nancy shuffled to the closed, metal double doors opposite her desk. "Are you related to Phyllis?" Nancy asked.

Keith shook his head. "I only need to speak to her. I promise not to take up too much of her time," he said.

"When you get to be our age, it's nice to have people to talk to."

With some effort, Nancy pushed open the door and stepped into a cavernous room, filled with card tables, bookcases brimming with paperbacks, a pool table, computer terminals, and a giant 70" flat screen television, surrounded by plush seating.

Though the room could hold over a hundred people, there were only a few milling around. Squinting over the top of her reading glasses, Nancy scanned the room. "There she is." She pointed toward the reading section. With a gentle pat on the back, she walked over to the bookcases with Keith following close behind.

"Phyllis?" she called, and Phyllis looked up and smiled.

Her blond hair still cut short, had thinned, and her fair skin wrinkled. She wore a stylish deep blue dress that matched her eyes. She turned to Nancy and glanced at Keith.

"Yes?" Phyllis said.

"This young man asked to talk to you."

"Oh?" She gave Keith a curious look.

"I need to get back to the front desk," Nancy said. "Have a nice visit, dear." She gave Keith another gentle pat on the shoulder before walking away.

Turning back to Phyllis, Keith said, "Sorry to bother you, Mrs. Udell."

"*Miss* Udell," Phyllis corrected with a stern tone. "Who are you?"

"I'm a friend of your daughter's," Keith said.

"My daughter?" Phyllis said incredulously.

"Yes, Lindsey. I'm trying to find her — "

"Who the hell are you?" Phyllis snapped.

"I'm Keith," he said.

Phyllis staggered backward a step as a gasp escaped her. She almost lost her balance and grabbed hold of a chair to recover. Her other hand covered her mouth.

"Keith?" she whispered, and her eyes glistened. "It's not possible."

He stepped forward, placing a hand on Phyllis' arm to help steady her.

"Are you okay?" he asked.

Phyllis only managed a nod.

"I didn't mean to startle you," he said.

"You can't be the one. You're just a baby."

"It was me she talked to on those tapes."

"You took your time getting here," Phyllis snapped, and Keith recoiled.

"I only found the first tape last week," Keith said. "I would have come sooner if I could."

"But how? She made those tapes so long ago."

"She said it was 1989."

"Were you even alive in 1989?" Phyllis asked.

"I was born in 1997."

"Then obviously it couldn't have been you."

"It was me. I don't know how Miss Udell. But when I played those tapes, she could hear me speaking to her across time, and I've traveled three-thousand miles to find her. Can you help me?"

After a moment, Phyllis nodded. "I can take you to her," she said. "Let me get my coat."

●

As they stepped out of the building, standing in the shade of the awning, Keith gestured to the parking lot. "My car is over here."

"That's okay, my driver will take us," Phyllis said, as a long, wine-colored Lincoln Town Car pulled along the sidewalk. The driver's door opened, and a diminutive man dressed in a black suit and cap hurried around the front of the car and opened the rear door for Phyllis. "Everything okay, Miss Udell?"

"I'm fine, Robert. This is Keith. He'll be joining me."

Robert bowed, tipped his cap and indicated Keith should enter the vehicle. Keith slid across the plush leather seat as Robert closed the door and hurried back behind the steering wheel.

"This is a very nice car," Keith said. "More room than my rental, for sure."

Phyllis didn't reply, keeping her gaze fixed out the window.

Keith's mind was spinning with a thousand questions. He was excited and curious, tempted to ask Phyllis a barrage of inquiries. But one look at her and he knew it would be a mistake. He tried to read her body language, but couldn't determine if she was angry, annoyed, or something else. He decided the best course of action was to remain quiet and enjoy the ride, knowing his long journey was finally ending.

Her driver traveled at a steady speed through town, careful not to jostle his passengers. He turned off the main road and headed up into the hills, covered in low, green shrubs, highlighted with ivy geraniums providing bursts of color.

They pulled up to the private entrance of a residential development, protected by a massive, ornate wrought-iron gate surrounding the community. The driver waved to an armed, uniformed man in the guardhouse. The gate swung open, and they passed through. Keith turned, to watch the gate close behind them.

He turned back towards the front of the car, stunned by the opulence of the homes. They were massive, multi-storied structures, with enormous yards of thick, flawless, emerald green grass, four-car garages and guest houses larger than his Aunt's home. It seemed Lindsey had done exceptionally well.

The driver pulled into a long, snaking driveway that looped around a multi-tiered fountain filled with cherubs spraying water on each other. The house was a Spanish style, with arched entryways, white stucco exterior, terracotta roof tiles, and red brick walkways.

Robert pulled to a stop near the front doors. He exited, rushing around to help Phyllis out of the vehicle. She stepped out with caution into the sunshine, and Keith thought she had aged on the ride.

Her driver opened the front door for her and waited as she climbed the steps, taking her time. He smiled and nodded at her as she passed, she didn't acknowledge him. Keith entered behind her, stepping into the grand foyer that reached thirty feet up to a cathedral ceiling where a wrought-iron chandelier glistened in the morning sunlight.

It was the most magnificent home Keith had ever seen.

A spiral staircase led to the second floor. Its railing dark, rich mahogany, buffed to a perfect shine. An enormous living room opened off the foyer, with a fireplace large enough for a man to stand in. A Mexican textile rug, in bright colors of red and blue, covered the floor.

Phyllis entered the living room but stopped halfway when she realized Keith was still standing in the foyer, admiring the stairs. "Join me," she said.

"Is this Lindsey's house?" he asked, as he stepped into the living room, stopping in front of one couch. Phyllis sat and gestured to him to do the same.

"This is my home," Phyllis said. "But Lindsey bought it for me."

"Is she here?" he asked.

"What did you expect to happen, Keith? Did you think she would be in some form of suspended animation, waiting for you like Sleeping Beauty? Didn't you realize the young woman on those tapes would no longer exist?"

"On the last tape, I promised her I would find her and I had to keep my word. I knew she would be older, but that didn't matter. It would still be her. From the instant I saw Lindsey, I knew she was special. She was unlike anyone I ever met before: smart, sweet, funny, and beautiful. But you know, you're her mom."

Phyllis nodded. "She told me about you. I didn't believe her. It seemed more like a coping mechanism for her loneliness, you know?" She looked at her hands, folded in her lap. "I insisted that she stop, for her own good, and she did. She went to college, studied, and got her degree. She did very well, and she took care of me."

"Is she here, Miss Udell?"

"Yes."

"May I see her? Please. I need to see her. Even if she has forgotten about me, I need her to know I kept my promise."

Phyllis' gaze shifted to the view of the valley outside the massive windows of the living room.

"Is she married? Is that why you are reluctant? I won't make any trouble. I want to see her, in person, just once. If she has a happy life now, I'll leave. I promise. Just please let me see her."

Phyllis stood, turned to the fireplace and walked over to it, then lifted an urn resting on the mantle.

She returned to the couch and sat, with tears welling in her eyes.

"I lost her to breast cancer, in 2008, Keith."

His mouth dropped open, his head shook, and the color fled from his face. He slipped off the couch, kneeling on the floor, his eyes fixed on the urn in Phyllis' hands, struggling to process what he had heard. A dull, ache permeated his body, as his mind reeled. He buried his face into the carpet, a sound of anguished pain escaped him, and the tears flowed, draining the life out of him.

The sound of his grief brought the staff into the living room. They saw Keith crumpled on the floor and Phyllis, seated beside him, holding the urn that once contained her daughter's ashes.

Phyllis indicated she was all right and asked them to bring a glass of water.

Keith struggled to his feet, wiping at his face, slick with tears and raw from the carpet, he mumbled an apology.

Phyllis rose, patting him on the arm and lead him back to the couch.

"Sit," she said.

Staring into space, feeling a complete disconnect between his mind and body, Keith complied. The shock, disbelief, and confusion brought a sense of déjà vu. It was how he felt after learning about his parent's car crash.

The housekeeper returned to the living room with a glass of cold water and handed it to Phyllis, who offered it to Keith. He took it without expression and drank.

"I'm sorry you traveled so far to receive such terrible news," Phyllis said.

"But I promised her," Keith said, his voice sounded thousands of miles away to him.

"I know you did. Lindsey believed you would, too. It broke her heart she wouldn't be able to meet you. But she gave me something and asked me to keep it safe. Wait here. I'll be right back," she said. She crossed the living room to the foyer and climbed the stairs to the second floor.

Keith worked to regain his composure. He wiped his face and ran his fingers through his hair, he wasn't sure what he looked like, but he knew it must be awful.

Phyllis returned carrying a shoe box, covered in colored construction paper, decorated with intricate illustrations. Phyllis sat down across from Keith, placing the box on her lap.

"Lindsey never doubted you would find her, Keith. She never wavered in that belief." Phyllis smiled, with a tinge of sadness. "It was a bone of contention between us. I told her it was foolish, and she told me there was nothing she was more certain of."

Keith battled back the emotions clawing inside of him.

"Towards the end, she gave me this box, and she made me promise to hold on to it until you arrived." Phyllis wiped away a tear. "Here you are, just like she always said." Tears flowed down her cheeks and dropped onto her dress. She handed the box to Keith.

He reached out to receive it, his hands shaking. As he took it from Phyllis, she smiled. Keith placed the box on his lap and then looked up at Phyllis, uncertain if he should open it in her presence, and then decided it was the right thing to do.

He removed the box top and inside was a small piece of paper with his name on it. As he picked up the paper, it revealed three other items below it: the two X-Men issues of *Days of Future Past*, and a videotape. Keith gasped when he saw it.

"I hope you have a way to play that," Phyllis said. "We got rid of the VCR's in the house years ago."

Keith nodded. "I do," he said his voice breaking. "Thank you, for keeping this for me. It means more than I can say."

"What kind of mother would I be if I didn't respect my daughter's dying wish?"

"Can you tell me about her," Keith asked. "Did she marry? Was she happy?"

Phyllis smiled. "Lindsey didn't marry. Never met the right guy, she said. But she was happy. She had a gratifying life and enjoyed great success."

"As an accountant?"

Phyllis snorted a laugh and then covered her mouth in embarrassment. "No, not as an accountant. She wrote and illustrated children's books. She was the author of *The Adventures of Oba and Nim.*"

Keith was thunderstruck.

"Do you know the book?" Phyllis asked.

Keith nodded. "My mom read it to me when I was little. And... I told Lindsey about it. But I thought Edith Kinsley wrote it."

Phyllis chuckled. "That was her nom de plume, an anagram of the names *Lindsey* and *Keith*. She told me you helped her with the idea. After the success of the book, she moved back to Hawaii. It was always her favorite place. She stayed there until the end. We scattered her ashes from a cliff on Oahu. I got to keep the urn."

They talked for half an hour, each sharing their memories of Lindsey. Then Keith excused himself and cleaned up in the washroom. When he returned, Phyllis was standing beside her driver.

"Robert will take you back to your car, Keith. It's been an eventful morning, and I think I need to rest a little."

Keith offered his hand. Phyllis surprised him with a warm and sincere embrace. He held her and whispered, "thank you."

She released him and stepped back. "Good luck to you, young man. Take care."

Chapter 25

Thirteen days had passed since Keith returned from California, but nothing had changed. Numb, shell-shocked, with his mind a tornado of depressing thoughts, he barricaded himself in the apartment.

Several times he'd picked up the first tapes from Lindsey, and tried to load them into the VCR, telling himself he'd feel better if he saw her smile again, or heard her laugh. But the grief was insurmountable. He never pressed the play button.

And the tape from Phyllis remained unwatched. He couldn't work up the courage to view it. The idea of speaking to Lindsey for the final time, while knowing she's already gone, was impossible for him.

So, he kept the shades drawn, lights off, and either stumbled through the rooms in a daze or stayed in bed, staring at the ceiling. Dressed in wrinkled, foul clothes, with mussed hair and a thick shadow of stubble covering his face, he resembled a madman, but he didn't care.

What's the point?

That was the stock response issued from his subconscious. Why bother doing anything? He was alone, and Lindsey was gone forever. He'd never get to hold her, kiss her, or tell her he loved her.

There is no point.

He opened his window and considered taking a header into the sidewalk. End it all. No more pain, no more misery, no more suffering. He climbed out on the sill, shivering in the frigid November air and sized up the fall.

With my luck, I'll only break my back and spend the rest of my life paralyzed.

He crawled back inside the apartment and closed the window.

Guilt gnawed at him, a relentless barrage of wondering why he couldn't have found her tapes sooner. But the more he dwelt on it he realized it wouldn't have changed a thing. When Lindsey died in 2008, he was eleven.

The whole thing was a nasty cosmic joke with him as the punch line. If there was a god, he truly was an asshole.

A pounding on the door pulled Keith out of his apathy and back into reality. He sat on the couch, motionless, hoping whoever it was would go away. Instead, the hammering intensified, and he heard Aric's voice outside the door.

"Keith, let me in. I'm worried about you. I've been calling for days, and your phone goes straight to voicemail. If you don't open the door, I'll find the superintendent and tell him I think you're dead."

Keith rubbed his temples, clenching his eyes tight. There was no escaping this confrontation. He had avoided Aric since coming back. Seeing him meant explaining what happened and re-living the whole horrible experience.

"I'm serious, dude. They'll come in with a cleaning crew and a body bag, only to find you wackin' it to porn, and won't you be embarrassed? Just let me in, man."

The deadbolt clicked back, and the door opened a crack. Through the opening Aric glimpsed only the hint of a form in the darkness and heard Keith's voice, raspy and dry.

"I'm not dead, okay. I want to be alone."

Keith tried to close the door, but Aric pushed his giant hand into the gap and opened the door wider.

"No, it's not. Listen, you jetted off to Cali and never even told me you got back. It's been almost two weeks, man. What happened? Talk to me."

In the darkened apartment, Keith closed his eyes and wished for an escape, but found none.

"All right," Aric said. "You need a little time, fine." He raised his other hand, holding a grease-stained brown bag, fragrant with fried peppers and onions. "I brought us grinders from Gino's."

Without waiting for a response, Aric pushed the door open and stepped inside. The grim conditions of the apartment were impossible to ignore. Clothes were strewn about, covering the floor, trash from takeout littered the room, and the air was heavy with the smell of body odor.

When Aric flipped the switch on the lights, it revealed Keith's condition. He almost didn't recognize his friend.

"Jesus," Aric said. "What the hell happened?"

Keith only shook his head.

Aric cleared a space on the couch and collected the clutter from the coffee table, bringing it to the trashcan in the kitchen which he found overflowing. He dropped it on top, making the pile bigger.

He came back into the living room to find Keith seated but staring off into space.

"Holy shit, you look like death warmed up," Aric said. He unwrapped the grinders from the bag and slid one over to Keith. "Eat something. You'll feel better, I guarantee. These sandwiches are like Prozac on a roll."

But Keith pushed it back.

"Fine," Aric said. "I thought I'd allow you to ingest high-quality comfort food before asking my questions. But if you want to forgo the eating and get down to the talking, I'm fine with that. What happened on your trip?"

Keith only stared at the table.

"What's the big deal? Tell me. I'm all ears. What's *so* bad you isolate your friends, barricade yourself in the darkness and refuse a grinder from Gino's?" Aric asked.

"She's dead," Keith said and failed to stop the flow of tears. He covered his face in shame and embarrassment. Aric moved close, placing a hand on Keith's shoulder.

"I'm so sorry," Aric said.

"I promised her I would find her, and when I did, it was too late." Keith wiped at his face, tried to compose himself. "I met her mom. She said Lindsey never stopped believing I would come for her. Before she died, she asked her mom to keep a package for me."

"What was it?" Aric asked.

Keith made a painful laugh. "Two X-Men comics and her final videotape."

"Did you watch it?" Aric asked.

"No."

"Why not?"

"It's unbearable. I can't do it. What am I supposed to say in my final conversation with the person I love? How does someone face that?"

"People have to do it all the time. I understand you're in pain. But she left this tape for you, Keith, and I think you have to watch it. It may provide closure. You can't stay like this," Aric said, gesturing to the apartment. "This isn't healthy, man."

Keith closed his eyes. "I feel like my soul's been ripped out."

"You should watch the tape."

"But what if I break down and she hears me sobbing? What if I say the wrong thing? *I'm afraid.*"

"She recorded it years ago, dude. Whatever happens, *she's already heard it.*"

Aric stood up, placing his sandwich back in the bag.

"I'll leave you now, and check on you in a few hours, okay? Watch the tape, Keith. It's what she wanted."

Keith nodded. He stood, and Aric wrapped his big arms around him, giving him a bear hug. "I'm here for you, buddy," he said.

Keith nodded. "You're a good friend, Aric."

"Go watch the tape."

●

Aric's words kept returning to Keith. Accomplishing closure was the essential step of the grieving process. After losing his parents, family and friends surrounded him at the wake. Each of them offering condolences, hugs, and handshakes, reassuring him he wasn't alone. The contact was comforting.

But for Lindsey, the news smashed into him like a runaway train. Blindsided by the grief, he had no opportunity to cope with it in the usual manner. To anyone who knew her, Keith was an outsider, a total stranger. Even if he'd attended her memorial services, no one would have offered him sympathy.

Keith wondered if watching the tape, seeing her one last time, might help close the gaping wound in his heart. Then he considered *could it be any worse?* The answer to that frightened him. He knew he teetered on the brink of oblivion. If things somehow got worse, it would consume him.

Considering what Lindsey had to say piqued his curiosity. What were her final words to him? How did she say goodbye? His desire to see her one last time was suddenly overpowering. He pushed back the devastation pulling on him like a black hole. Keith removed the lid of the box Phyllis gave him and admired the beautiful markings made by Lindsey's hand. He picked up the videotape, decorated with the same ornate details on the label. Written in the center, with her perfect penmanship, it said *"For Keith,"* and his hands trembled. He sensed a subtle tingle of energy from the tape pass into his fingers. The gentle vibration continued along his arm and through the rest of his body, warming and calming him. He placed the tape into the adapter and slid it into the VCR.

He closed his eyes, took a breath, and pressed the play button.

The monitor flickered, replacing the static on the screen with a breathtaking view. Wide windows overlooked a pristine beach of white sand with turquoise waves breaking across them in a spray. Through the speakers, Keith heard soft footsteps off camera, and then a woman stepped slowly into the frame.

It was Lindsey.

She was older perhaps in her forties. Despite the dark circles below her eyes and hollowness in her cheeks, he recognized her instantly. Streaks of gray highlighted her long, black hair. She smiled and opened her arms. All he could think was she still looked beautiful.

"Hi, Keith. You found me. I always knew you would."

Keith stammered.

Lindsey raised a finger to her lips. "Please, don't say anything. If you speak, I'm afraid I won't be able to go through with this."

He nodded and allowed her to continue.

"I don't know how to tell you, so I'll just come straight out with it. This is the last video I'll ever make for you. I want you to remember me as I am, not as... I don't... I don't want you to see me... fade."

"Lindsey, please, let me be there for you. I want — "

Her chin trembled, and she held up her finger, stopping Keith. "I've known for a while now, and I've kept it from you. I didn't want to... to make it real. You were always my escape, somewhere I could go to hide from reality. But, reality, I guess, has a way of catching up to you. By now you know what has happened to me. You understand what I'm talking about. You know the name of the dragon whose talons grip me. I won't say the word... not to you." A tear slipped down her cheek, and she forced a smile.

Keith wiped at his eyes.

"Before I go, I want to say thank you, Keith. Thank you for being there with me my whole life, for believing in me... for loving me."

"Lindsey," he whispered, fighting the tears.

"Don't cry. You've made me happier than I ever thought I could be. And you helped my dreams come true. So it's my remaining wish to do the same for you. To make you happy, be there for you, and believe in you all your life. And love you, unconditionally and always. That's why I've left something for you. I've left you me, Keith. I've left you *us*. Go find it. I promise I've made it easier this time."

"I don't understand," Keith said. "What does that mean?"

Lindsey lifted a piece of paper and held it close to the lens, revealing a phone number. "Can you see this?" she asked.

"Yes, but — "

"Call the number," she said. "Tell them who you are."

"Wait, Lindsey, don't go, please," he sobbed. "*I love you.*"

"I love you too, Keith."

And then the screen flickered to snow.

Chapter 26

Hoboken, New Jersey
November 9, 2019, 5:21 PM

Keith sat in front of the video monitor with the tape paused on a frail-looking Lindsey holding up a phone number. *What could it be?* Embarking on another quest was both thrilling and frightening to him. It felt like getting a second chance, but was he up to the task?

He dialed the phone with shaking hands. Maybe the number connected to an answering machine with another message from her.

The call answered on the second ring.

"Attorney Daninhirsch's office, can I help you?" said a young man's voice.

Keith felt a flash of disappointment not hearing Lindsey's voice. He took a moment to regroup. "Um, yes, hi," Keith said. "Lindsey Hale told me to call this number. My name is Keith Nolan."

"One moment, please."

There was a click, followed by a Muzak version of "Eternal Flame." His mind struggled to comprehend why Lindsey asked him to call a law office.

The line clicked again interrupting the music and his thoughts.

"This is Attorney Daninhirsch, with whom am I speaking?" said the voice of an older woman.

Keith cleared his throat. "My name is Keith Nolan."

"How did you get this number, Mr. Nolan?"

"Lindsey Hale told me to call it?"

"She *told* you?"

"Well, she made a videotape for me, and at the end, she held up this number and said to call it."

There was a pause, and Keith heard shuffling papers.

"I have a few questions I need you to answer," she said.

"Ok, but what is this about?"

The lawyer ignored him. "What were your parent's first names?"

"Why do you need that?"

"It's necessary to confirm you are who you claim you are before we proceed further. These are questions Ms. Hale required me to ask."

"But I don't think I ever told her my parent's names."

"Just answer the question, Mr. Nolan."

"Arthur and Louise."

"Your best friend's first name?"

"Lindsey wouldn't know that. I never talked to her about him."

"His first name?"

"Aric," Keith said.

"And finally the last name of your favorite writer."

"Claremont."

"Excellent," she said. "It's nice to speak with you after all this time, Mr. Nolan. I will require you to visit my office at your earliest convenience to go over things."

"Where is your office?"

"Los Angeles," she said.

"What? I'm in New Jersey."

"Yes, I'm aware. I'm authorized to provide you with air transportation to LAX and a driver will then bring you to my office."

"What the hell is this all about?"

"I'll explain in person, Mr. Nolan. If you tell me when you'd be ready to travel, I'll have a ticket waiting for you at Newark Liberty International Airport."

Keith looked down at the food stains on his t-shirt. "I will need to shower first."

●

The flight to California passed in a blur. Keith had never traveled first class before and it astonished him to find the seat bigger and more comfortable than the recliner in his apartment. As he sank into the soft padding, his mind whirled. Grief continued to gnaw at his consciousness, but it was offset by curiosity as he worked to unravel Lindsey's mystery.

"I've left you *us*."

What did she mean by that? He didn't know, but the promise of it filled him with excitement and anticipation. When the plane began its final approach into Los Angeles, Keith couldn't believe over four hours had passed.

A driver, dressed in a black suit and holding a card with Keith's name, greeted him as he descended the escalator to baggage claim.

"May I take your bag, sir?"

"No, thanks," Keith said. "I got it."

The driver led him out of the airport to an idling Lincoln Town Car. Keith slid across the plush leather seats as the driver closed the door, walked around the front of the vehicle, and got behind the wheel.

"First time in L.A.?" the driver asked as the car pulled away from the curb.

"No. It's actually my second time in a month."

"Oh. You must rack up the frequent flyer miles. Are you here on business?"

Keith shrugged. "I'll let you know when I find out."

The driver chuckled and navigated onto the 405 Freeway. A haze hung over the city. "Traffic is heavy, per usual. I'll do my best to get you to your destination as soon as possible."

Thirty minutes later they arrived at an impressive office building of silver and glass on Sunset Boulevard in Beverly Hills. The driver parked the car and then came around to open the door for Keith.

"My instructions are to wait here for you," he said.

Inside the lobby, Keith told a receptionist he had an appointment with Attorney Daninhirsch. She instructed him to take the elevator to the fifth floor. When the doors opened, a young man greeted him.

"Mister Nolan?" he asked.

Keith stepped out of the elevator and onto plush carpeting. He admired the elegant office decorated with black leather couches and tables of silver and glass.

"Yes," Keith managed.

"I'm Dave, Attorney Daninhirsch is expecting you."

He led Keith to a corner office overlooking Sunset Boulevard. Seated behind a mahogany desk was an attractive older woman, impeccably dressed in a black fitted jacket and matching skirt. She smiled and rose as Keith entered.

"I'm Isabella Daninhirsch."

"Hello, I'm Keith Nolan."

"Please have a seat," she said. "Has Dave offered you anything to drink?"

"No thanks," Keith said. "I'm good. I'm just wondering what this is all about."

Isabella dismissed Dave and sat back down behind her desk. "I need to see two forms of identification, please. Driver's license and a credit card will suffice."

Keith looked puzzled, but removed his wallet and extracted the cards, giving them to the lawyer. She looked them over, nodded, and then handed them back.

"I was Lindsey Hale's attorney for over twenty years. I negotiated her book deals, handled her finances, but more than that, I considered her a friend. When she was coming to the end of her life, she asked me for one final service. She told me about you, and asked me to promise that when you contacted me, I was to give you this." She handed Keith a sealed manila envelope.

"What is this?"

"Open it," she said.

Keith ripped it open, and a set of keys slid out onto the desktop. Checking the inside, he noticed a document and removed it.

"That is the deed to her home in Hawaii. She wanted you to have it."

Keith could only blink in disbelief.

"There is one requirement. The property has a groundskeeper who lives in the guesthouse. You must allow him to remain as long as he wishes. His monthly pay and any expenses are handled through my office. Do you have questions?"

Tears welled in his eyes. "She gave me her home?"

"Yes, she did. If you sign these papers, stating you agree to the terms of the arrangement, I'll have your driver bring you back to the airport. There's a ticket waiting," she paused, smiled and gave a shake of her head. "Sorry, she told me to say it just like this: 'to take you to paradise.'"

•

By the time Keith arrived on the island of Oahu, he had traveled almost five-thousand miles, across six time zones, all in one day. His head was buzzing and his senses tingled. Hawaii was everything he imagined and more. Palm trees swayed in the tropical air, warm and fragrant with a blend of sea and flowers. Craggy cliffs with cascading waterfalls and the endless hypnotic sound of the ocean waves mesmerized him.

A different driver, an island native, named Don, drove Keith from the airport to Lindsey's estate, in the Waikane Valley, on the eastern shore of the island. After about twenty-five minutes on the freeway, they turned off onto a private road and traveled through thick, lush vegetation. They arrived at a security gate decorated with ornate metal sculptures Keith identified immediately. It was Oba and Nim, the Hope and Dream, from Lindsey's book.

Don rolled the vehicle beside a call box outside the gate and pressed the red button. They waited almost a minute before the speaker crackled with the voice of an older man.

"Can I help you?"

"Yes," Don said. "Mr. Keith Nolan is here."

There was another pause, and then a buzzer sounded as the gates opened and the car drove through. The beauty of the property stunned Keith. Its landscaped grounds were breathtaking, but nothing could prepare him for the reveal of the residence.

The structure was octagonal, three stories high, with a continuous deck surrounding the perimeter of each floor. It was built on top of a rocky cliff overlooking the ocean. Gardens of wildflowers, ornamental grass, and volcanic rocks, encircled the house.

"Not too shabby," Don said with a chuckle as he parked the car at the main entrance.

Keith couldn't speak. He was in awe.

The main doors opened, and an older man stepped out on the deck. His hair was thin, but his eyes were bright and clear. As Keith exited the vehicle, he thought he recognized him somehow.

As Don removed Keith's bags from the trunk, the man stepped down from the deck and extended a hand.

"You must be Keith," he said.

Keith shook his hand, surprised by the strength of the grip. "I am."

"Lindsey told me a lot about you. It's nice to meet you finally. I'm Nick, the groundskeeper, and her father."

Keith's eyes widened. "It's nice to meet you, sir."

Nick laughed. "Forget that *sir*, stuff. I work for you now. Wanna see the place?"

The inside of the house was as impressive as the outside. Its shape and design provided vast open spaces, with stunning views from every location. On the first floor, Nick walked him through the living room, dining room and a massive kitchen.

"If you like to entertain," Nick said, "you could accommodate a small army in here."

For the first time in two weeks Keith managed a laugh. "Unfortunately, I don't know many people."

The second floor had the bedrooms and baths.

"Before you explore those, I want you to see the top floor," Nick said with a smile.

The third floor was Lindsey's work studio. Desks, worktables, and easels littered with art supplies filled the space.

Dozens of her sketches and paintings decorated the walls. Keith's eyes welled as he tried to take it all in. Her essence permeated the room from every corner. "They're beautiful."

"This was her favorite place," Nick said.

Keith moved through the space in reverence. "This is where she worked her magic," he said in a hushed tone. "Her pictures, her tools, they're all still in place. It's... it's like she's still here."

Nick nodded. "She made me promise to keep everything just how she left it for when you arrived." He shrugged. "She said that would be important."

He approached her primary workspace, a vintage roll-top desk, and spotted a framed illustration set prominently beside her sketch pads. It was a drawing of a young man who bore a surprising likeness to him, along with a hint of Brad Pitt, and an impressive abdominal six-pack. Keith couldn't help but chuckle.

Near the windows facing east was a sectional sofa and stacked behind it were dozens of storage boxes filled with comic books. Keith's mouth hung open as he realized it was a complete run of Uncanny X-Men.

"Lindsey, you were perfect," he whispered and couldn't hold back the tears as the pain of losing her, again overtook him.

Nick shifted uncomfortably.

Keith noticed and wiped at his eyes as he regained his composer. "Sorry," he said with a sniffle.

"This must be overwhelming."

"And then some."

"I have one more thing left to show you," Nick said.

He led Keith down to the second floor. On the landing, he gestured to three open doors. "There are three guest bedrooms, all clean with fresh linens if you want to invite anyone over. I stay in the guesthouse at the back of the property. There's a direct line, if you need anything, call."

Keith nodded.

Nick walked down the hallway to a closed door, and Keith followed.

"This is the master bedroom. It was Lindsey's room," he said. "She left something for you inside. I will give you some privacy."

"Thank you."

Nick managed a sad smile. "We all miss her, Keith. But it means a lot that you are here." He chuckled. "You know, I never really believed it, all those years. I thought... I thought it was just her imagination. She really was something special, something magical, wasn't she?"

Keith could only manage a quick nod as he tried to hold back the tears.

Nick smiled, walked away and descended the stairs. Keith turned back to the closed door, with his heart hammering in his chest.

In his head, he heard Lindsey's older voice.

"I've left you *us*."

He reached for the knob and opened the door.

The bedroom was bright and spacious. Dressers and a walk-in closet lined one wall. Against the other was a queen-sized bed that faced the western windows and the setting sun. At the foot of the bed was a massive, antique steamer trunk. On top of it sat a sheet of paper with something written on it. He stepped closer to inspect it.

For Keith.

Along the edge was an intricate lattice illustration.

Tenderly he moved the note to the bed and opened the trunk. He gasped as he saw its contents. *Hundreds* of videotapes filled the chest. Each numbered and organized with a detailed label illustrated by Lindsey's hand.

He dropped to his knees, sobbing.

She never stopped recording.

After several moments he pulled himself up and sat on the edge of the bed. As he gazed into the trunk, he noticed a small piece of equipment off to the side. He reached out and picked it up. It was a portable playback unit with a built-in display. When he pressed the power button, he expected the batteries to be dead, but instead, the screen illuminated.

He took the top tape from the stack, removed it from its case, and slid it into the player.

After an instant, the screen flickered to life and revealed a daytime view of the massive Sequoia forest where Lindsey recorded the sunrise. A moment later she stepped into the frame. She was young again, vibrant and so alive.

"Hello, beautiful," he said, doing his best to hide the quiver in his voice. "It's *so* good to see you."

She beamed. "I can hear you!" she said and giggled. "That's fantastic news. It means you found this tape even though I'm keeping it. That guarantees we meet in person someday," she said with a silly grin and laughed.

"I promised I would find you," he managed.

"And I knew you would, Keith. I felt it in my heart. That's why I kept making these tapes. But instead of you having to dig through a dumpster to find them, I'll keep them safe and give them to you in person, whenever that day comes. I can't wait to see you."

Tears streamed down his face.

"I'm sorry how things ended on the last recording. At the time I was upset and thought I should move on. But then I realized how stupid that was. I couldn't give you up, so I won't."

"That makes me so happy," he said, his voice breaking.

"Are you ok, Keith? You sound upset."

He cleared his throat and sniffed. "Yeah, I'm fine."

"Listen, I know there's this issue of time between us. But I don't care. You're in a different time now than me, but that will change someday. Until then, you are with me here." She placed her right hand over her heart. "Always and forever. No matter what happens, okay? You are the sweetest, most considerate guy I've ever met, and I'll wait for you however long it takes. In the meanwhile, I'm going to build my future, and I'll share it with you on these tapes."

"What's the plan?"

"Well, I'm taking accounting classes at the community college like my mom wanted, which made her happy. But guess what?" she said, bubbling with excitement. "I was at the diner nearby, having a cup of tea and drawing in my sketchpad, when a woman stopped and praised my work."

"That's fantastic," Keith said.

"That's not the *good* part," Lindsey said. "Turns out she's a literary agent who represents a writer looking for someone to illustrate her book. The agent requested a portfolio of my work!"

"Congratulations," Keith said with sincerity.

"Well, I doubt anything will come of it, but it's sure nice to dream, right?"

"Lindsey, if you believe in yourself, the way I believe in you, you will never fail."

"See, that's why I need to keep talking with you. You boost my confidence. How are you doing with your imagination? Have you tried that technique I told you about?"

"I tried," he said. "But there were too many distractions."

"Why don't you try it again?" she asked. "Close your eyes and imagine you are here with me, among these beautiful trees, on this perfect day."

"But if I close my eyes, I can't keep looking at you. And that's all I want to see," Keith said with a tremble in his voice.

"Don't be silly," she said. "Use your *imagination*. Come on, try it."

With reluctance, Keith closed his eyes. "Okay," he said. "But this doesn't work for me."

"That's your logic brain talking. Forget about that and focus on *me*. Whisper the magic words."

With his eyes closed, Keith whispered, "*Sail to serenity. Sail to serenity.*"

"Now, picture this place in your mind," Lindsey said. "Imagine you are here, beside me on this rock. Feel the warm breeze on your skin. Hear the wind whispering through the branches."

In Keith's mind, the image appeared. He saw the dark brown bark of the massive trees, and the camera on its tripod with its red light flashing. "It's working," he whispered.

"Now feel me putting my arms around you," she said.

And he did.

She was there in front of him. Her eyes sparkled, her skin glowed, and her long hair flowed.

"Can you see me?" she whispered.

"I can," he cried.

"Now kiss me," she said.

And he did.

Special Thanks

Thank you for taking this journey with me. I'm grateful you selected to read my book over the countless other entertainment choices available to you. That means a lot.

I'd love to hear your thoughts about the book; you can post comments at MichaelKHill.com or send me an email at Mike@MichaelKHill.com. I look forward to hearing from you.

Please consider leaving a review on Amazon. They're extremely helpful in getting readers to try a novel from an unknown author.

If you enjoyed this book, it's because of the wonderful work of *many* people.

David Taylor, my editor, played an absolutely indispensable role. His feedback and suggestions made the book better in every way.

A huge thanks to Noly at TheArtsyReader.com for all of her valuable help. I am forever in your debt.

Friends and family:

Elle Bucko, Tracy Thielman, Michael Hand, Amy Castolene, Beckie DiGiovancarlo, Robbie Mills, Laura Carter, Rit Carter, David Hirschler, Martha Rein, Rachelle Cardone -Hill, Tiana Cardone-Hill, Nick Hill, Gail York, Anne Checovetes, Jackie Cheney, Gwen Brady, Michael Brady, Tim Reed, Shelly Sampon, Morey Amelotte, and Susan Lesley Stewart

Your help as beta readers, sounding boards, and sometimes therapists is invaluable.

Thank you, Rita Mikulak, for the love of reading.

Fellow writers and mentors:

Louise DiMeo, Arthur Groth, Arthur Macabe, Alex Hareland, Joseph Michael, Stephanie Barbé Hammer, Effrosyni Moschoudi, and the original RedditWriters

I've learned so much from you all.

Thanks to Alexandra V. at Kingwood Creations

Thank you to the online communities that assisted in so many ways:

Everyone at NaNoWriMo.org

Zoetic Press and the *Write Like You're Alive* FB group

The incredible people of:

r/books, r/KeepWriting, r/PubTips, r/Scrivener, r/selfpublish, r/writers, r/writing

The gang at r/comicbooks was a huge help.

In particular:
u/AbraxasWasADragon
u/Eric77TA
u/kissmybacon

Literature and Latte
Jason Louro and Campfire Technology

Thanks for making amazing software for writers.

Very special thanks to my Mom and Dad for *everything* they have done.

And finally, thank you Beth.
Without you this wouldn't have been possible.

Michael K. Hill
May 17, 2019

Made in the USA
Middletown, DE
28 July 2019